D1374236

Unless Recalled Earlier
DATE DUE

Himalaya

Himalaya

by JONATHAN NEALE

Houghton Mifflin Company
Boston 2004

Copyright © 2004 by Jonathan Neale

www.houghtonmifflinbooks.com

The text of this book is set in Mendoza.

ISBN-13: 978-0-618-41200-6
ISBN-10: 0-618-41200-X

Library of Congress Cataloging-in-Publication Data

Neale, Jonathan.
Himalaya / by Jonathan Neale.
p. cm.
Summary: In alternating chapters, twelve-year-old Orrie and her older brother
tell the story of a doomed mountain-climbing expedition in which they,
their younger brother, their divorced father, and his girlfriend
attempt to climb Island Peak in Nepal.
ISBN 0-618-41200-X
[1. Survival—Fiction. 2. Mountaineering—Fiction. 3. Brothers and sisters—Fiction.
4. Divorce—Fiction. 5. Himalaya Mountains—Fiction.] I. Title.
PZ7.N27Hi 2004
[Fic]—dc22
2004000973

Manufactured in the United States of America
MP 10 9 8 7 6 5 4 3 2 1

For Michael Szpakowski

Author's Note

Those who know the mountains of Khumbu well will notice that I have moved one mountain for this story. Other than that, this is pretty much how it is up there.

One

Into the Mountains

Orrie

I don't know if I can find the words to tell you how beautiful those mountains are. But I can tell you what happened to us, and what death looks like.

Two days before we left for the mountains I woke up in the middle of the night. A voice in my stomach said, "Chocolate hobnob cookies. Chocolate hobnob cookies." The display on my glow-in-the-dark clock said 2:15. But I could not disobey the voice. I went downstairs.

I didn't turn on the lights. I didn't want to wake anyone. I wasn't ashamed of sneaking the cookies. The way I see it, if you need comfort food, eat it.

I'm twelve years old and I'm having a pre-life crisis.

I went into the kitchen and saw the red eye of a cigarette glowing. Behind it was the shadow of my mother's face.

That's really why I tried to be quiet. When Mum wakes up, she never gets back to sleep. I didn't say anything to her. I just opened the fridge and took out the packet of cookies and sat down at the table with her.

Chocolate hobnobs never taste as good in my mouth as they do in my mind. I'm going to have to stop eating them. I can't afford to get fat. My family is embarrassing and my head is full of dangerous ideas. I need every edge I can get.

"Why do you keep the hobnobs in the fridge?" I asked Mum.

"Cookies hate the heat," Mum said. "If they get too hot it reminds them of the oven where they were born, and they get homesick."

Mum always has a reason.

"Why do you grind your cigarettes out like that?" I asked. She was screwing her cigarette down into a saucer full of butts, really leaning into her wrist, smashing the cigarette down. We were going away to the Himalayas with my dad in two days. They're the biggest mountains in the world. I was worried about how Mum would cope while we were away.

"I imagine the saucer is the face of my enemy," Mum said.

"Does it work?" I asked.

"You mean like when you meet them the next day, they have burns all over their face?" Mum said. "And they've applied lots of Band-Aids to cover the marks? But you know they're there, and they don't know you know?"

"Yes."

"No," Mum said. "It doesn't work like that. But it gives me great personal satisfaction."

After Dad left, Mum hung a dartboard on the wall of her bedroom and put Dad's photograph over the bull's-eye. We used to hear her throwing darts in her room late at night.

"Can I do it?" I said.

"No," Mum said. "Smoking is bad for you."

"Not smoking. Can I grind one out?" She had already lit another. There were like twenty butts in the saucer, and some had spilled out onto the kitchen table. She must have been sitting there a long time.

"When I finish this one," she said.

I sat there and had another cookie. That made three, which is 300 calories. I wondered who Mum's enemies were. Did she have like twenty different enemies? Or did she stub a cigarette out on the same face twenty different times? I didn't ask, in case she told me. I didn't want to know who her enemy was.

I put the cookies in the fridge to stop them from staring

at me and screaming, "Eat me!" I got another saucer from the drainer so I had a clean one of my own. I waited. Mum handed me the cigarette. I looked down at the saucer and tried to imagine Libby's face. Libby is Dad's girlfriend in New York. Suddenly I could see her face on the saucer in the dark. I ground the cigarette out right in her eye. I messed it around on her eyelids too, so all her eye shadow ran down her face. She uses dark blue eye shadow to highlight her big blue eyes. She's years younger than Dad and uses too much makeup. Mum was right. It gave me great personal satisfaction.

None of it is Libby's fault. I do know that, really.

"Can I do it again, Mum?" I said.

Mum went and opened the fridge. When she bent over the light inside lit up her face. She's a beautiful woman. Mum took a tomato out of the fridge and put it on the table. She pointed a long finger at the tomato and said, "My enemy's head." Then she made her right hand into a fist and held it above the table. She smashed her fist down on the tomato. Red stuff squirted everywhere.

I went and got my own tomato and put it on the table. "Libby's head," I said under my breath, so Mum couldn't hear. I smashed it.

Mum got two tomatoes and lined them up next to each other on the table. "Both my enemies," she said. Mum brought both fists down at the same time, which is harder than it looks. *Squash, squish,* and we laughed up a storm. When we'd used up all the tomatoes, I got Mum upstairs to bed. As I tucked her in, she told me about Dad's letter.

Jack

When I came downstairs this morning the kitchen was a mess. There were like ten dirty coffee cups on the table. There was a saucer with maybe twenty cigarette butts in it. The kitchen smelled. And it looked like someone had been smashing up tomatoes all over the kitchen. It must have been my mum and my sister, Orrie. They do strange things in the middle of the night.

I do all the cleaning up around here. Someone has to be the grownup. I'm thirteen, and it's me. Other guys have the kind of mothers you see on television. I know. I've been over to their houses. Charles Cresswell and I work on his computer in his room, and his mum comes in with a mug of tea for each of us. She says there's nice fresh muffins she just baked, too, with homemade raspberry jam. I say, "Thank you, Mrs. Cresswell." She says, "Call me Fiona." Charles says "Umphh" and stuffs the muffin in his mouth without looking at it. He never takes his eyes off the computer screen. Later we can hear Fiona vacuuming the hall outside. Charles is my best friend. But some days I think I'd kill him if it meant I could get his mother instead of mine.

I didn't say that. I didn't even think it. I love my mother. But you have no idea how hard it is to get tomato gunk off kitchen walls. What were they doing in here, to get tomato bits on the walls? It's a good thing we've been taken out of school because we're going to the Himalayas tomorrow. I hate having to clean the house and then be late for school. It's such a dumb excuse. "I'm sorry, sir. I was late because I had to clean the house." Girls laugh at me.

They must have used thirty tomatoes. As I cleaned, I ate all of Orrie's chocolate hobnobs from the fridge. It will be a learning experience for her when she comes downstairs and finds they're not here.

I don't feel I'm any less of a man because I do all the cleaning. My dad did all the cleaning when he lived with us. So I have a role model. All the same, when Charles comes over I don't let him see me cleaning. But that's because he teases me. I don't think people should tease their friends.

Orrie came downstairs, her face all bleary. I was standing on a chair, scrubbing at a bit of dried tomato gunk up near the ceiling. "Sorry," she said.

"So like what happened?" I asked.

"You don't want to know," she said.

"I do. I want to know."

Orrie was standing in the doorway. Somehow bits of tomato had got stuck to my face.

"Mum got a letter from Dad," Orrie said. "He wants us kids to go live with him in New York when we get back from the Himalayas."

I fell off the chair.

New York is magic. But Mum can't cope if we leave her. She has mental health problems. She'd probably have to go back into the hospital and spend the rest of her life sucking her own drool. I love my dad. His girlfriend, Libby, would clean up after us. I've seen her do it. We'd be normal. But I also love my mum. How could I choose between my parents?

Orrie helped me up. My elbow hurt from falling on it.

"What do we do now?" I asked.

"Like I know," Orrie said. She learned to talk like that in New York. We're half American and half English. Dad's the American, Mum's the English. Dad went back to New York and left us in England.

Our little brother, Andy, walked into the kitchen with a five-foot boa constrictor snake wrapped around his neck. Andy is only seven years old. So we had to change the subject.

"Where are the kittens?" Andy said.

"Boa can't play with the kittens," I said. Boa constrictors kill their prey by wrapping their coils around it and squeezing until the animal suffocates.

"Why not?" Andy asked.

"It's a rule," I said. I'm bigger. My word is law. I'm trying to take care of everybody.

Andy's face scrunched up. "You think Boa will kill the kittens," he said.

"No," I said.

"He won't," Andy said. He had his sincere face on. He's a really cute kid, all eyes and freckles.

"He eats mice," I said.

Boa slithered around Andy's neck. The muscles moved under the snake's skin. It's orange and black. "He only eats dead mice," Andy said. "And he doesn't do that any more."

"Too right," Orrie said. Orrie's a vegetarian. She made Andy stop feeding Boa dead white mice. Andy used to hold them by their tails and dangle them in front of Boa's nose. A boa constrictor can unhinge its top jaw from its bottom jaw and make its mouth into a humungous hole. He just sort of gulped the mice. Watching Boa eat mice was like watching a car wreck. You can't watch and you can't take your eyes away either. The bulge of the mouse moves down inside the snake. You can see it. The stomach acid slowly eats away at the mouse in there. I'm glad Orrie stopped all that. Now Boa eats canned cat food like everyone else.

I didn't want Boa to start eating the kittens. You'd have to put your hand in there and pull the kitten out. And get greasy snake saliva all over your hand. Plus, the kitten would already be punctured or have its back legs broken or something. Then what would you do with the kitten? Knock it on the head with a hammer and put it in the garbage? While Andy watches? Or give it back to the snake? Probably there'd be one of those endless funerals in the backyard where Orrie reads poems and Andy cries all the way through. And I'd have to dig the hole.

"What makes you think Boa won't eat the kittens?" I asked.

"He promised me," Andy said.

The mountain we're going to climb is called Island Peak. It's 21,450 feet — really high. The ice is so white, Dad says, the glare will hurt your eyes if you look directly at it. So we'll be wearing ski goggles. Dad knows what he's doing, and we'll be careful.

We're getting credit from school for this. Mum went in and made all nice to the head teacher. Mum's a pretty good talker, and it turned out the head's a climber. We have to keep journals and write a report when we get back in December. The head told the whole school in morning assembly. Everyone's really envious. I'd better get to the top.

We'll figure out what to do about Mum and living with Dad when we get back.

My elbow's probably broken.

Orrie

I looked after Andy's snake while he and Jack played with the kittens. Boa coiled round my arm, watching the kittens with a fierce black eye. His tongue flicked in and out, tasting the air. That's how snakes locate the animals they kill.

I haven't made up my mind what I'm going to do when I grow up. Maybe I'll be a singer. Then I could have a big boa constrictor on stage that wound round me as I sang. People would really notice that. It would be like my signature. I'll call myself Orchid. Lots of singers have just one name. And Orchid's my real name — my parents were hippies. Maybe I could wear a sort of orchid costume with my snake.

Our cat Muppsells has eight kittens. They've only just opened their eyes, and they still look sleepy, but so interested, seeing everything for the first time. Andy sat on the floor and the kittens tumbled over each other, falling off his lap. Two of them climbed his shirt. They dug their little claws into his cheeks and went for the top of his head. They sat there on his hair, holding on with their claws, looking around at the world.

There were tiny drops of blood on Andy's cheeks. He didn't make a sound. Andy has this thing with animals. It's like he can talk to their souls. I think he's a fairy who's been sent to live with us.

Muppsells sat next to Andy and never took her eyes off

me and Boa. I should have taken Boa into the next room. But I didn't want to be alone with him, in case something went wrong and Andy wasn't there to rescue me.

Dad didn't really leave on account of Libby. He left because Mum's a Hula-Hoop. I don't think you leave someone because of that. I think you should stay and look after someone with mental difficulties. Dad says he only met Libby after he left us. I think that's true. Dad wouldn't lie to me. It's hard to live with crazy people. Anyone who wants to marry me, they're going to have to take a personality test first.

Mum came into the room rubbing her hands together. She does that when she wants to show people she's taking charge of her life.

"How's everyone doing?" she asked.

"I hurt my elbow," Jack replied. Andy didn't say anything. I think he was worried that if he moved his mouth the kittens would fall off his head. But his eyes were dancing. He loves Mum.

For lunch Mum made us pasta with yogurt and raisins on top of lettuce, just the way we like it.

"Who's looking after the kittens when we go to the mountains?" Andy asked.

"Me," Mum said.

"You'll have to give them away while we're gone," Jack said.

Andy looked at Mum. She nodded. Andy tried not to cry.

"It's better to tell him these things," Jack said to me.

"I didn't say anything," I said.

"Think how he'd feel if he just came home and found out," Jack said.

"I know that," I said.

Andy rubbed his eyes with his fists. After all, he's only seven.

"You have to give kittens away when they're six weeks old," Jack said to Andy. "They're old enough to leave their mums then, but they're still really cute. So people take them because they forget they turn into boring cats."

"What about Muppsells?" Andy said. "She'll worry."

"She'll worry," Mum said. "But I'll talk to her. Two old ladies together, missing their children."

"I've been reading this book about French climbers in the Himalayas," Jack said. "They got to the summit of Annapurna and got really bad frostbite on their toes. They couldn't walk, and the Sherpa porters had to take turns carrying them down the mountain. Each Sherpa carried a big Frenchman in a basket on his back. They came to a great cliff with a tiny ledge across it. The Sherpas had to turn and face the rock wall and inch along it sideways. The Frenchmen in the baskets hung out over the drop."

Jack stood up to show us. He got me to climb on his back and be the Frenchman with frostbite.

"You haven't finished your pasta," Mum said.

"We're only showing you," Jack said. He began walking sideways along the kitchen wall, me clinging to his back. His fingers looked desperately for a hold on the flat wall. I looked down at the thousand-foot drop to the river below.

"Don't move," Jack said, "or I'll fall."

I let out a little moan.

"Shh," Jack said. "Don't break my concentration."

I froze on his back, silent. It seemed to take hours. Jack got to the corner of the wall. I jumped off his back. Andy clapped. Mum looked scared.

Jack sat down and dug into his pasta. He talked with his mouth full. "All the way down the valley the doctor had to keep cutting off their frostbitten toes," he said. "Because the toes were dead and turning black and gangrene was setting in. When they finally got to the railway station, one of the Frenchmen looked at the holes where his toes had been. He saw a little yellow maggot peeping out of every hole." Jack wiggled his fingers in front of us like little yellow maggots.

"I don't want Andy to go," Mum said.

"It'll be OK, Mum," Jack said. "I know what I'm doing."

"Oh, great," Mum said.

"Mum!" Jack shouted.

We all looked at our plates. My pasta looked like little yellow maggots.

"I wanna go with Jack and Orrie," Andy said.

Dad and Libby came to get us from Mum's the next day. Andy cried. Mum cried straight into Dad's face. Jack pretended he wasn't crying. Libby and I didn't cry. I hated her for it. I don't want to talk about it.

We went to Heathrow Airport and took the plane to Kathmandu, in Nepal, the country where the Himalayas are. We had to change planes in Kuwait, with an eight-hour wait, and then again in Delhi, with a six-hour wait. Libby sat on the airport floors with Andy and read him *The Cat in the Hat*. She was trying to look good. Dad told Jack and me all about Nepal and the Himalayas. He went there before with Mum, when they were both young hippies, before we were born. I think he's doing all this so he can get back to where he was happy.

We came into Kathmandu, the capital of Nepal. We walked right out of the airport and into the sunlight. Dad got us a taxi. On the ride into the city I fell in love. Not with a boy. With a whole country.

The streets are full of people walking every which way. There are monkeys and dogs and there's a haze of smoke over everything. The women's clothes are beautiful. Red and orange and stripy, and saris that start out dark blue at the top and just sort of change color so you can hardly see it, till they're light, light blue down by their feet.

We have to wait in the city for three or four days while Dad gets all the official permission for the mountain we're going to climb. From the roof of our hotel you can see the Himalayas to the north. Jack and I go up there every night and look out over the city while the sun sets. There are swallows, I think they are, dipping through the air — and bats. On the far hill across the river you can see the monkey temple.

The street kids give me the jibbers. They look so poor. Their clothes are rags and they have sores on their faces. The boys come up to me and whine till I give them money. I don't like it. Dad says I should carry lots of little coins with me so I can give to the beggars. But never give to the kids, he says, they just never stop asking if you do.

I don't pay any attention to that.

One of the beggar boys showed me everything he's been collecting after I gave him some money. He has this big torn plastic bag on his back, and a pointed wooden stick. He looks through the streets for bits of plastic, spears them, and puts them in his bag. He has empty Coke cans and empty fish cans and bits of cardboard, too. His name is Ganesh. He sold me a picture he'd made with crayons, of himself collecting plastic. I gave him thirty rupees, which is sixty cents. I know it's too much, but who cares.

Dad says Ganesh can sell all the bits of plastic in his bag. People are poor here, Dad says, so nothing really gets thrown away.

Today I went out to find Ganesh. I saw a smiling policeman beckon Ganesh over. You could see Ganesh was scared but thought maybe the policeman had something for him. Ganesh got close and looked up at the policeman. He's a pretty small kid. The policeman hit Ganesh in the mouth as hard as a grown man can hit a kid. Ganesh flew across the street backwards.

I hate myself because I was too scared to do anything. I went back to my hotel room and hid. The hotel has wall-to-wall carpets and marble floors in the bathrooms. Dad says he used to stay in the hippie part of town but now he's breaking Libby into the rough life gently. She just smiles and slaps his arm playfully when he says that. They make me sick.

Today we're flying to Lukla, an airstrip in the mountains. From there we will walk up to Khumbu. Khumbu is the name of the valleys around Everest, the highest mountain in the world.

We were stuck in the Kathmandu airport for hours and

hours. They had to wait for the clouds to clear at Lukla. Then suddenly it was all go. The Nepalis were hurrying to get through a little door onto the airport tarmac.

The Nepalis on our plane were Sherpas, people from the mountains with sort of Chinese faces. The women wear big black dresses and aprons with red and yellow stripes. There were even two bald old Buddhist monks in long robes like dresses. One of the monks was wearing a jacket with a Nike swoosh but he'd dyed it orange to match his robes. The monks had trainers and rucksacks. So did the little old ladies.

The plane had rows of two seats on one side and one seat on the other. It held about twenty people in all. A cabin crew woman offered us sweets. I took four. The door to the cockpit was open. I was right near the front. I could see the pilots and all their instruments and right out the pilots' front window.

We took off. I looked out my side window and Nepal was spread out before me. The land is all green hills dotted with houses. There are fields on almost every part that isn't a cliff. From up here it looks like each field is a step in an endless staircase.

We were flying high and the mountains came up to meet us. Suddenly we were only a couple hundred feet above the top of a hill. I could see a path, and people carrying packs. I waved to them, and the plane began to bounce up and down in the air. I looked at Jack in the seat in front of me. He was staring straight ahead, gripping the sides of his seat. I looked behind and Libby smiled at me, a sick little smile, and I knew she was scared, too. I'm not scared of anything. It was like being the most powerful bird in the sky.

Libby said, "Look," and pointed out the window. I looked and saw great mountains on our left, floating above the clouds, very near and cold and white.

The clouds came down and covered us. The plane bucked. We dodged in and out of the clouds. I watched the pilots, their hands easy on the levers above their heads that controlled the plane's altitude. Suddenly a wall of green trees was coming at us from out of the clouds. The pilots pulled on the levers and we jumped up and soared over the wall. I could hear Jack being sick into a little bag. I won't tease him about that. I looked round for Andy. He was sitting beside Libby, and I could tell he didn't know what to think. So I threw him a smile of crazy joy. Andy gave me one back, a real mouth splitter. All over the plane you could see the Sherpa women praying, the little worry beads sliding through their fingers, and mumbling in fear. I guess they know these planes. But to die like this would be to die in heaven.

We turned hard to the left. There was a steep slope

almost next to us, nearly straight up and down. Too steep for fields. Some bits were rock cliffs, and around them pine trees clung to the sides. We went down into the clouds again.

The plane turned, went all the way round, and then turned back. Now even the men were praying. I felt a strange wild wanting, I don't know for what. Laughter bubbled up from my tummy. I held it back, or people would think I was mad. All around was cloud. We were in a deep, narrow valley and could go straight into either side. Then the cloud opened through the pilots' window, and there was the Lukla airport coming up at us.

It's not really an airport. It's a landing strip laid into the mountainside. There are no flat places around here. So when you see the landing strip coming at you, it looks impossibly short and angles steeply up the hill. It would be so easy to smash into the ground. The pilot and co-pilot were talking calmly to each other. We hit the airstrip and bumped. There was a great rushing sound of the plane's brakes. Then we were up the hill and everyone was cheering.

Jack

We had a bit of a bumpy ride on the plane to Lukla, which I didn't much like. Then we were out, on bare ground.

Orrie told me she wants to be a pilot in Nepal when she grows up, which is completely unrealistic.

They got us off the plane quickly, so they could load it right up with more people and take off while there was still a hole in the clouds. Dad met up with his old friend Anu. Anu is going to be our *sardar* — the Sherpa who takes us up the mountain and looks after everything. He had two porters with him. They took Orrie's and Libby's packs. I held onto my pack when they tried to take it. I'm like Dad. He carries his own pack.

Then, with no tea or anything first, we set off along the path into the mountains.

Orrie

The Himalayas came rushing down through my eyes and mouth and nose and took my heart away, to be forever theirs.

The air smelled of pine trees and mountain streams and the electricity before a storm. It was thin air up here. Always after each breath I wanted a little more. But always I felt this was more air than I had ever had. The real air, before they put the crap in.

I stumbled and fell on the path, banged my knee and scraped my hand. Five minutes later I fell again. Kersplat, big pain, and up again. The path was rocky up and down, and you had to pick your way and watch your footing. But all I wanted to do was look and look and look.

The bottom of the gorge was maybe a thousand feet below us. Everywhere the pines marched up the hillsides. They were not forests. Every tree stood on its own, clawing up to the sun. Long green mosses dripped from the branches, like the beards of the grandfathers of fog. The clouds cleared and the sky was the crayon-blue little kids use to color it. You can't see the great mountains but you know they're there, round the next bend, or the next. The valley we were in was so deep and narrow that the sides cut off the view of anything else.

The path went down and the river came up to meet us. White water from the glaciers rushed round the great rocks. The path was full of people. I smiled at them as I passed, and everyone smiled back. They carried heavy loads suspended by straps across their foreheads. The straps held big wicker baskets that they carried on their backs.

One woman carried a whole basket full of cans of Coke. A boy not much older than me was carrying live chickens piled on top of each other and clucking like mad. He had a portable radio tied on top of his basket. There was that wailing Indian film music coming from the radio, and the chickens were yelling. I danced to the music as I passed him, and he danced behind me, as best he could with the weight, and sang the radio song. I was way in front of my family, running on ahead, running to my true home.

There were huge boulders in the middle of the path, as tall as a house. Some ancient people had carved Buddhist letters a foot high on the boulders. Nowadays the local people have painted the different letters orange and yellow and blue, so the letters leap out at you. I think the colored letters make prayers.

By the side of the path, stretching up the hill, are the Buddhist prayer flags. The flags are on ropes that are strung between poles, trees, rocks, with dozens of flags in each row, blowing in the wind. The flags are the same colors as the letters, plus green and red, with writing on them, and there's a picture of a man on a horse in the middle of each flag. The writing is a prayer, Dad says, and each time a flag flaps in the wind, that prayer goes up to heaven for the person who put the flag up. So one person can pray a million times a day. Neat.

Jack

My pack's pretty heavy. I think it must weigh twenty pounds. But I managed to keep up with Dad and the porters. Orrie went running on ahead, because she didn't have to carry anything. Libby held Andy's hand so he didn't slip. She's nice. Orrie says Libby's trying to look extra good and caring to show Dad she can be a good mother if we go live in New York. Maybe so, but it's still nice. Of course I would never want anyone to replace my real mother. When I walked behind Libby, her long red hair swished back and forth across the black shirt she was wearing.

We all stopped for a rest outside a little teahouse. They had benches by the path, made from big flat stones. We all took off our packs and relaxed in the weak sun. It's pretty cold up here in October. Dad lay down and went right to sleep. He can do that anywhere.

Andy bought a packet of Nepali biscuits from the tea-house. Libby told him to give one to each of the porters. They said "Thank you" in English. I got one, too. Nepali biscuits aren't chocolate hobnobs but they taste pretty good after a hard walk.

When he thought I wasn't looking, Andy gave a biscuit to the dog who's been following us since the airstrip at Lukla. It's a black dog, normal size, with a stick-up curly tail, a white snout, and white front paws. He gulped down the biscuit and looked up at Andy with hungry eyes. Andy gave him another biscuit.

"Don't do that, Andy," I said.

"Why?" Andy asked. He gave the dog another biscuit.

"He'll follow us all the way to Base Camp," I said.

"So?" Andy said. He leaned over and patted the dog's head. The dog licked his hand. It probably had fleas.

"So?" Libby said.

"He has a family," I said. "They'll miss him."

"He knows where his home is," Libby said. "There's only one path here. He'll go back home when he's ready."

Andy gave the dog another biscuit. I saw the look on the face of one of the porters. These porters are poor people. He was wearing clear plastic shoes, and it was cold. I bet he was thinking he didn't have money to buy biscuits, and this little white boy gave four to a dog and only one to him. I wanted to say this to Libby and Andy, but I was too embarrassed.

Libby was patting the dog. "What's his name?" she asked Andy.

"Cookie Wolf," Andy said.

I put my pack on my back and walked away, leaving the others behind.

Orrie

Last night we stayed in a village named Monjo. The hotel was a big old stone house with wooden floors. Each room had just two beds and a mattress. Andy and Jack shared a room and I had one of my own. We had noodle soup and Andy played with the little kids who lived in the hotel.

Cookie Wolf had to wait outside the hotel in the cold. Andy took him some bread to eat.

Dad got out his map and showed us all where Island Peak was. Again. He keeps doing it. It's up beyond Gokyo, ten days' walk north of here. He told us again it was 21,450 feet high.

He laid the map out on the table and we all looked at it. "Tell her, John," Libby said quietly to Dad.

Dad just flicked his head.

"Tell her," Libby said.

Dad looked at Libby like, Shut up.

"She has a right to know," Libby said.

"Let's go out and look at the moon, poppet," Dad said to me.

We put on our down jackets. They make you look like an Eskimo, but they're twenty times as warm as an ordinary coat. Mine is bright red. Dad's is blue. We went outside. The moon was almost full and the clouds drifted across it. We could hear a stream close by, the water pounding the rocks, and could smell the spray in the air. It was too cold to stand out there long. It gets bone-crunching cold up here once the sun goes down. You can see your breath even inside.

Dad hunched his shoulders so he kind of looked broken-down. "Orrie," he said.

Uh-oh.

"I'm afraid you won't be able to climb Island Peak," he said.

I just felt strange all over. "You promised," I said.

"It's too dangerous for children in the mountains," he said.

"Jack's still going to climb the mountain," I said.

"Jack's older."

Jack is one year older than me. "Jack's a boy," I said. "That's why."

Dad just stood there, his shoulders all pulled in. "I'm sorry, Orrie."

"Libby's going up the mountain, isn't she? Because you love her. You're just making me the babysitter. She wants me to stay with Andy so she can climb and not look after your slimy little kid." I stopped talking then, because I would have cried.

Dad turned his back on me. Then he made himself face me. "Orrie," he said, like he was begging, but for what?

I left him there and went up to my cold room.

A few minutes later someone knocked on my door. I didn't make a sound. They weren't going to see me cry.

Libby opened the door and said quietly, "Orrie?"

I turned my face away. She sat down on the side of my bed.

"Orrie," she said in her fake gentle voice, "I'm going to stay down at Base Camp with you and Andy."

Dad had told her what I said. He made her come say this.

"I don't need you," I said.

"Getting to the top of things isn't what life is about," Libby said. "That's what men think. We'll stay at Base Camp and look at the beauty, not try to conquer it."

"He'll leave you when he's finished with you," I said. "Just like he leaves everyone else."

That got her. She left the room without a word. If I'm mean enough I can make Dad take me up the mountain. I hate being mean to Dad. He just wants me to love him.

Jack

Orrie was really upset. After Libby came downstairs I waited about twenty minutes. Then I went up and sat on Orrie's bed and held her hand. That's how we do it. I don't say anything, and it's safe for her to cry. After a while, I went back to my room and lay in the dark and thought.

I haven't told anyone, but after Island Peak I'm planning to come back in two years' time and become the youngest person ever to climb Everest.

Libby has a younger sister. I wonder how old she is. Maybe she's my age. I lay in bed and thought about the sister. The same long red hair, the blue-green eyes, the cute crooked nose. Of course her sister would look younger. Would her breasts be as big?

Her sister and I don't meet until after I climb Everest.

She's pretty impressed. I let her feel my muscles. She gives me a foot massage. I hope this is all right. Imagining your dad's girlfriend's sister isn't wrong. I think.

She licks my toes.

Orrie

Today we walked up the Namche Hill. That's the long hill, two thousand feet high, that takes you up to Namche Bazaar, the biggest village in Khumbu.

It was a long way, really steep. I was out ahead as usual, huffing and puffing. I didn't want to be with the rest of them. I'm not talking to Dad. Dad's Sherpa friend Anu came with me. He didn't ask me if I minded. He was just there, not too far from me. I think he's worried about me being a girl on my own. That's sexist. I think he can see I'm unhappy, too.

The pine trees all around meant you couldn't see much. The hill just went up and up. Yesterday the path was mostly rock. Today it was wet dirt, so I was slipping and sliding. We passed a man carrying a whole tree trunk on his shoulder, maybe twenty feet long. The path kept switching back and forth. When he came to a turn the man had to stop and steady the log. It looked like if he leaned back another six inches it would pull him over backwards to his death.

"Hard life," Anu said.

I stopped a bit farther up the trail, where there were some stone benches. Anu sat next to me. I offered him some of my water. He held the bottle over his face, opened his mouth, and poured the water in. His lips never touched the bottle. I guess it's cleaner that way.

"Why can't I climb Island Peak?" I asked.

"It's dangerous," Anu said.

"I'm not afraid," I said.

"Trekkers die up there," Anu said. "Every season, one trekker dies. Sometimes more. Climbers die, too. And Sherpas." Trekkers are the foreigners who walk on the paths. Climbers go up the high ice-covered mountains. "Last season, four foreigners died, all trekkers, not climbers. From altitude sickness. All big people, not children." He was looking straight at me, trying to force me to understand. "I do not want a child to die," he said.

"Did you tell Dad not to let me climb the mountain?"

"Yes. I am the sardar of the group. My job is to take care of the group. My child died in these mountains."

"Where?" I asked.

"Here," Anu said. "Years ago. My son was bringing firewood from the valley. He fell. I was away working for an expedition. My wife told me when I came home three months later."

"How old was he?"

"Your age."

I don't think he knows how old I am. "Why did you tell Dad it was safe for Jack to climb the mountain?"

Anu looked at me. His eyes were black and old. He is the sort of man whose eyes do not lie.

"You told Dad not to take Jack," I said.

Anu didn't nod his head and he didn't look away and he didn't say anything. He just kept talking to me with his eyes.

"Why don't you make him leave Jack at Base Camp?"

"I work for your father," Anu said and looked away.

"So what?"

"I need the money." Anu turned his back in shame.

Dad is going to take Jack up the mountain even though Anu says it's dangerous. Anu's been to the South Col of Everest, almost to the top. He's an old man. He's a Sherpa. He knows what he's talking about.

Last year we got lost with Mum on a small boat in the middle of the Atlantic Ocean, and Dad was frantic when he found out what had happened. Now it's like he doesn't care if his kids die. It's because Jack is so desperate to climb a mountain. Dad thinks that if he doesn't let Jack climb, Jack won't love him. And then Jack won't go live with Dad.

Dad's right, too.

Jack

Dad and I walked up the Namche Hill together. I got pretty tired, but I didn't say anything. I could see Dad was puffing, too. It was nice just being with him.

Dad stopped to rest with his chin on his walking stick. We have matching walking sticks we bought at a little tea-house by a waterfall yesterday. They're made of wood, and strong, but they bend a little as we walk. Local people made them. You meet a lot of foreigners coming down the path with two metal ski poles, one in each hand, all brightly colored. They don't look right for these mountains. And the people look funny walking with two sticks, like old insects. One wooden walking stick, that's the right way. Dad's been here before. He knows.

I went and peed off the side of the path. It was also the top of a cliff. It's fun watching your pee fall five hundred feet. When I got back, Dad asked me what color my pee was. What kind of a question is that?

"Purple," I said.

"Seriously," Dad said.

"Seriously purple. Deep purple."

"Really," Dad said.

"I didn't look," I said. I had looked, but I wasn't looking at the color. I didn't want to explain all that.

"Clear, sort of white, is good," Dad said. "Yellow is bad."

"You've spent too much time in America. Now you're

worrying about toilets like them." I don't like my dad talking to me about my pee. Who knows what comes next?

"This is about safety, Jack."

"Safe urine?" I asked, and Dad gave me a lecture about altitude sickness. He said the higher you go, the less oxygen there is in the air. That means the body tries to breathe more quickly, to get more oxygen in. But the more quickly you breathe in, Dad said, the more carbon dioxide you breathe out. And the more carbon dioxide you breathe out, the sicker your body gets. So your body makes you stop breathing quickly, and you don't get enough oxygen. After a few days at each new altitude, your body adjusts. The way you can tell if you've adjusted is if your urine looks clear and transparent. That means you're OK. If it's yellow, you're in trouble.

"OK, Dad," I said. He seemed pretty worried.

"People die, Jack." Dad said that if you don't get enough oxygen, the brain gets sick. You get a terrible headache and lose control of your muscles. You just flop all over the place. Sometimes the altitude sickness gets into your lungs. Then they start to fill up with fluid. You can drown with as little as a cup of liquid in your lungs.

Dad said about half the people who come up here get mild altitude sickness. They get headaches and have trouble sleeping. That's because every time they go to sleep, their bodies want to breathe faster. But another part of the body wants to slow down and gives an order to stop breathing. So you stop. Luckily, you wake up immediately and start breathing again. But you don't know what happened, and you're scared, and you don't know why you're scared. And you wake up right in the middle of a dream, scared, so you remember your dreams vividly and they all feel like nightmares. So you think nightmares are keeping you awake all night long.

"That's all normal," Dad said. "You don't have to worry if that happens. But you shouldn't go any higher until you're all right."

"I'll be fine, Dad."

He looked even more serious. "The people who die," he said, "are the people who are trying to be brave. Most often it's a middle-aged man who's the slowest in the group. After the day's walk, he's the last one into camp at night, and he's puffing. People ask him if he's OK. He says yes because he doesn't want to look weak. In the morning he's dead."

"I'll tell you," I said.

"The other ways you can tell," he said, "are if the little moons at the bottom of your fingernails turn blue. That means you're not getting enough oxygen." We looked at the moons of our fingernails. They were white, not blue.

35

"They say kids are more likely to get altitude sickness."

"That's silly," I said. I'm not a kid anyway.

"One theory is that altitude sickness increases the pressure in the fluid around the brain. Kids' skulls are smaller, so there isn't as much room for the fluid, and that squeezes the brain." Dad looked so worried. "Are you sure you want to climb Island Peak?"

"Yes."

"Maybe it's not a good idea."

"I told the whole class I was going to climb the mountain."

"You'll tell me if anything's wrong?" he said.

"They'll tease me, Dad. Please."

He looked at me with a strange expression I didn't understand. Then he said, "OK."

"Thanks, Dad."

"We'll all be careful," Dad said. He sounded sad.

"I'll be careful," I said. And I will, too. I'll watch my pee and my fingernails. But I better be careful what I tell Dad. If he gets worried about me, he won't let me climb the mountain.

People worry too much about their children.

Orrie

Anu and I came round the corner, out of the trees, and

there was the village of Namche Bazaar, above us. Namche is in a steep bowl. The houses march up the hill, spreading out in a horseshoe shape. The walls of the houses are thick stone, and the wooden shutters are painted bright blue and yellow. Colored prayer flags snap in the wind on the roof of every house. It's a place of magic, a fairy-tale village in the mountains.

At the edge of the village the path went through a small arch, where it was cool and shady. They had painted gods, demons, and Buddhas on the walls and ceiling. Beyond the arch was a square building with no doors, as tall as six people. On each wall someone had painted a single massive eye in orange and black. Anu said it was the eye of Buddha, so you know God is always watching you. Anu takes his religion seriously. The building is called a stupa. It was built in the old days, when there were only five families in Namche and men went to get water in groups because they were afraid of the bears.

Then we were in the village of Namche itself. The path changed to flat paving stones, making narrow village streets with steps up everywhere. There was ice on the stones, and we had to take every step carefully. Little shops sold Tibetan jewelry, rucksacks, and climbing gear. The streets were full of shaggy yaks, some carrying loads and some just standing, chewing, and looking dopey like cows.

We came to a thick wooden doorway and went into a dark corridor. Anu said this was our hotel. I stepped into a room full of light. The whole opposite wall was one big picture window filled with a view of the rock cliff of Kwangde Peak. The cliff of Kwangde is six miles wide and it rises six thousand feet from the valley we started from this morning. The black rock is full of shining waterfalls frozen into ice.

This is my spiritual home. Anu went into the kitchen to talk to the Sherpas who run the hotel. I sat by the picture window and looked at Kwangde and ate a Mars bar. I got talking to some men who were staying in the hotel. They said they were Austrians taking a break from trying to climb a terribly hard mountain called Lhotse, right next to Everest. There were three of them, really fit lads in shorts, with legs as thick as a man's body. Their faces were dark red, with pale white where they wore their goggles on the mountain. They looked like raccoons with beards. I wanted to tell them about the mountain we're going to climb. But I didn't, because now my family won't let me climb it.

Then Dad and Jack and Libby and Andy and both porters turned up. It was all hullabaloo. Everyone said how tired they were and how tough they'd been and how much meat they were going to eat.

Except Andy. He said, "Want to come talk to the yaks with me and Cookie Wolf?"

38

We sat among four yaks tied up in the field below our hotel. Two of them were black and white, two were orange, and all had thick tangled wool. Andy told them all about our life back in England, and they nodded a lot. Cookie Wolf sat off to one side. Yaks have big curved pointy horns, and I don't think they like dogs.

Andy sat with me and Anu at supper. I asked Anu about the musical horns I can hear coming from across the village. He told me it was a funeral. Two old people from the village, a man and a woman, both got sick and went to the hospital in Kathmandu. The doctors told them they had cancer and there was nothing they could do. So the two old people came home to die. They had cancer in different places in their bodies, Anu said, but they both had it.

They died yesterday. Anu said this was bad. He can't remember a time when two villagers died on the same day. They weren't related or anything.

The monks blow the horns. When someone dies, the monks come to the house for two days. Some of the monks make music. Others sit the body up in a corner of the house, and the person's old friends come and say goodbye to the body. The wisest monk sits next to the body for two days and reads to the dead person from an old book. The book tells the body how to find its way around in the land of the dead. That way the person's soul won't get trapped there. And it won't go to one of those places where you get reborn as a bad animal, like an ant or a rat. With the monk reading the book to it, the dead person can find the place where he or she gets reborn as a human baby.

"Can we be reborn as yaks?" Andy asked.

"Sometimes," Anu said.

"Can I go to the funeral?" I asked.

Anu's face went angry.

"I'm sorry," I said.

"Funeral is not for tourists," Anu said.

"I'm sorry." I was so ashamed.

The music of the horns is lovely, though, sad and loud.

Jack

I kept waking up all night. The same dream, over and over. Amanda, this cute blond girl at school, found out I hadn't climbed a mountain. Amanda has these perky little breasts and blue eyes that dance in the light. She was laughing and pointing at me. The other girls were giggling. I knew where Amanda was pointing. I looked down and saw I was so ashamed that I'd pissed my trousers.

We have to wait in Namche for three days to get our bodies used to the altitude before we go any higher. But it helps to walk up to a higher place each day to get your body adjusted. Climb high, sleep low, they say. This morning

Orrie and I walked up the hillside together. We needed time to talk to each other.

We climbed up the steep path between the fields, slipping and sliding, and got to the ridge above the village. There was an empty field full of prayer flags on ropes slung from one rock to another. We sat down on one of the rocks and split a Mars bar I bought in the hotel. I don't like buying chocolate bars here. They cost a hundred rupees. That's more than half what a porter earns for a whole day's work. I don't want any of the porters to see me eating one. But they taste like home, and that makes me feel better.

"I've been thinking about eating meat," Orrie said. She has a big Meat Means Murder poster on the door of her room back home. I didn't say anything.

"They eat yaks up here," she said.

I had a grilled yak sizzler for supper last night. It came on an iron plate, still bubbling in its burning fat. It cost 180 rupees. There weren't any porters in the room to see me. It sure tasted good.

"The monks eat meat, too," Orrie said.

"Yes." I'd been surprised. Back home Buddhists are vegetarians.

"It's because animals have a life up here," Orrie said. "Look at the yaks in the fields, running around playing with each other. It's not factory farming."

"Yes." I didn't want to sound too enthusiastic or gloating. She might change her mind.

"I won't eat meat when I get back home."

"No," I said.

"Anu says he told Dad you shouldn't climb the mountain."

My body tightened. The world went blurry.

"Anu says he had a son who died when he slipped on the path round here, carrying wood. He doesn't want to see more kids die."

"I'm not a kid."

"Anu says it's not safe for people our age to climb."

"You're lying," I said. "You're just jealous. That's all you are. Dad said you couldn't climb and now you want to ruin it for me."

"Jack."

There were five or six wild mountain goats behind Orrie. Their blue-tinged wool coats brushed the ground as they leaned down to chew the grass. Their horns were long and twisted.

"Jack, Jack." She was begging me. A big billy goat on a rock high above stared down on us, keeping guard on the herd. Orrie didn't see the goats. She was all caught up in her lies.

"Dad stopped me going because Anu told him to," Orrie

said. "But he's letting you climb. 'Cause he thinks if he doesn't let you, you won't go live with him in New York."

Orrie was just saying whatever she knew would hurt.

She's very damaged, my sister. I left. I walked on up the hill, pounding my feet into the path, breathing hard. I'll show them how fit I am. All around the path are juniper, little twisted green pine trees that don't grow as high as me, because of the wind and the cold. They smell like heaven, a thick redwood scent. I sat by a juniper, alone.

Orrie

I shouldn't have said that. I let Jack go.

I sat on the rock for a long time, watching the wild mountain goats all around me. Jack hadn't seen them. There was one big mommy goat high up on top of a rock, keeping watch to make sure the little goats were OK.

I hate it when Jack argues with me. He's my only real best friend in the world. Tessa back home is sort of my best friend. But I can't really talk to her about my family. Jack's been through it all with me.

I walked down the hill into Namche. I saw smoke in the distance. There was a rocky space cut into the side of the hill, far away. A man was standing there, looking out. I think it was Anu. They were burning the bodies from the funeral. The smoke swirled round the man. His shoulders

43

were square, but somehow his body was sad. It was like he was waiting and the bodies were taking a long time to burn. The sky was turning gray above the smoke, the clouds coming down. The land was yellow rock and green juniper. It was a beautiful death.

Cookie Wolf met me on the way down the path. We found Andy and Libby sitting with some more yaks. Andy wasn't talking this time. He was just sitting by the yaks, wearing his little red down jacket and his blue woolly hat. He had his legs crossed under him like Buddha does in the pictures. Libby was sitting off to one side.

"What's he doing?" I asked Libby quietly.

"He says he's listening to the yaks eat."

The yaks ate. I tried to listen. I didn't hear anything. Cookie Wolf sat down next to me and I put a hand on his fur.

"How's Jack?" Libby whispered.

"Fine."

"He was looking a bit sick this morning."

"He's fine."

"Isn't Andy cute?" Libby said. "I'd love to have you all come and live with us."

I turned away and started petting Cookie Wolf.

"It's up to you," Libby said. "Whatever you want to do. But it would make your dad happy."

"You're not my mother," I said.

***

I'm going to wait until the rest of them start up the mountain. A few hours later I'll start up on my own. By the time I catch up, we'll all be so high they can't turn round. The thing about sexism is you have to fight it.

Jack

This morning we set out from Namche for our mountain, Island Peak. We're going to spend five days walking up to Gokyo. Dad says we could do it in two or three. But you're only supposed to sleep twelve hundred feet higher each night or you get altitude sickness. So each day we have to stop after a few hours of walking. In Gokyo we have to wait two more days. After that we walk across a glacier and up to our mountain. Then I climb it.

Dad doesn't want to spend a lot on porters. He wants us to do this all on our own. Anu has found someone to take our extra stuff up to Gokyo on yaks. From there we'll be on our own, carrying our tents. Dad says this is a wilderness, not a campground.

The path the first day was cut into the side of a steep hill. The drop below went three thousand feet down to the narrow gorge of the Dudh Khosi, the same river we've been following since the Lukla airstrip. The path went up a bit, then down, then up and down some more. There are no flat paths in Nepal. I walked behind Dad.

Orrie

Andy and me were racing along in front. Anu was keeping up, looking after us. Libby follows Andy everywhere. It's like she's practicing to be a mum.

What if Dad has more children with her?

There were a lot of yak trains on the path. Each yak carried two heavy bags, one on each side. They were ferrying supplies up and down to the base camps for the expeditions. Sherpas walked along with the yaks, guiding them. A lot of them were boys and girls our age. I smiled at them and they smiled back.

The yaks kept trying to stop work and wander off the path and up the hillside to eat grass. I saw one girl herding yaks. Her lead yak wandered off the path. She threw a stone at the yak as hard as she could. But she aimed for the horn, not the body. She hit it, too, with a loud crack. The yak jerked back and shook his head. Then he got back on the path. I'm going to learn how to throw like that. I won't practice on yaks, though.

Anu told Andy and me to be careful. He says yaks sometimes turn on the person who looks after them, even if they've known each other for years. But mostly how people die is they try to pass a yak on the outside of a narrow path like this. The yak doesn't care about you one way or the other. It just comes down the path like a tank and pops you off the path with its shoulder. Doesn't even know what it's doing. You fall three thousand feet and you're ketchup.

Cookie Wolf is wary of the yaks. He never barks or misbehaves or runs around like a normal dog. He's part of life here. So he behaves in front of the other people and animals.

We went round a corner and there was a yak lying on the path. It had long orange fur and a white stomach, and its feet stuck straight up in the air like a cartoon animal that's dead.

I didn't want to get too close. I wasn't sure it was dead. The eyes were open and swollen and crazy. The head and horns were twisted to one side like it had fallen and broken its neck. The stomach was swollen like it was full of death gas. But there was no smell.

Andy went right by me. I grabbed for him and missed. He sat down by the yak's head and looked into its staring black eyes. Then he began stroking its stomach and talking to it. I moved round the yak, very carefully, and sat by Andy.

"It didn't hurt, did it?" Andy said to the dead yak. "It's scary in the land of the dead, you know? You have to be careful. Don't rush around in the land of the dead. Don't open the wrong door. If you go through the wrong door, you get born again as one of the wrong things — a snake nobody likes, or a big kid who hits people."

Andy was talking real quietly, like Mum talks to me when I've had a nightmare. Gently, her voice making everything safe.

"It's dark in the dead land," Andy said to the yak. "If you run, you bang into things. You get more scared. Just sit at first, Yakky. Sit there and talk to yourself. Sing yourself a little song. Remember playing with your friends when you were little. Remember the first time you tasted grass."

Where did Andy learn all this stuff? Libby was sitting beside me, and Anu sat behind her. I didn't look at them, but I knew they were there.

"Now look around, real slow," Andy said. "Real quiet, Yakky. You can see little bits of lights from behind the doors. You can go up to the doors any time you want. And open them. When you go through, you come back into the world. You'll be in some mummy's tummy then. Pick a good mummy. Pick a good door. Don't run. Rest first. Then go to a door. And listen. Behind the bad door, you hear shouting. Grownups arguing. Don't go through that door. Move on. Behind the good doors, you hear mummies singing. Go through that door, into the song."

"Orrie," Jack shouted from behind us, "I can see Everest!"

Anu ran back to shut up Jack.

Jack

I came round the corner and there it was: Everest, the highest mountain in the world. You could just see the black tip of it poking over the Nuptse ridge in front. There was a plume of snow blowing off Everest. There always is. It's so high, the top is in the jet stream and the wind always blows.

I've seen hundreds of pictures of Everest. This time was for real. The thing you can never see in the pictures is how big everything is, how high the mountains, how deep the valleys.

Spread out in front of us were dozens of mountains. Between and below was the green of the steep valleys. Right in front of us, miles away, was the village of Phortse, sloping fields hanging to the side of a mountain.

Orrie was messing around with some dead yak. I yelled at her to come look at Everest. She gave me her piss off look. I hate it that she's not talking to me.

Anu came immediately to look at Everest with me. He's a wise man, and kind. I want him to like me. I want him to let me climb.

Dad came up and looked at it with us. "There was a bitter storm on Everest six years ago," he said. "About thirty people were trying to reach the summit that day. They were tourist climbers, in parties with guides. No way did they deserve to be up there. The Sherpas do all the route

49

making, climbing the hard bits of ice, carrying the supplies on their backs. The Sherpas put up fixed ropes and the tourists just clip on and walk up."

I looked at Anu on the other side of me to see if he agreed with this. His face showed nothing.

"The summit day some of them were short-roped," Dad said. "That means the Sherpa ties a rope round the climber's waist and drags them up the mountain."

I looked at Anu again. He nodded to me.

"They were just coming down from the summit when the storm hit," Dad said. "The European guide stayed at the South Summit with a dying climber. The others suddenly had to fend for themselves. They froze to death all over the place. The funny thing is, one of the survivors wrote a bestseller about it, and since then twice as many people come to Khumbu. They're excited by death."

I didn't tell Dad I'd read Krakauer's book, too.

"It is good for Sherpa people," Anu said. "We have work." He was talking to Dad over my head.

Dad didn't know what to say back. So I asked Anu, "Have you ever climbed Everest?"

"Yes."

"What did you feel at the summit?"

"Nothing," Anu said.

"Weren't you pleased?"

"I was cold. Afraid. Wanted to go down. The member wanted to take photos. Of me, of me and the flag, of me taking photo of the member holding the flag. Member kept saying this is fantastic, Anu, fantastic. I said we go down now or we die. Member said, only a few minutes more, Anu. He was always saying that."

"Member" sounds so weird. It's what Anu calls climbers. It's what he calls us, too. It means a member of the group, but he only uses it for foreigners. "Why didn't you make the member go down?" I asked.

"Member is boss," Anu said.

"Did the member die?"

"No."

There was something about how Anu said no that made me ask, "Did anyone die?"

Anu nodded.

"Who?" I said.

Anu looked away. I knew it was a Sherpa.

"That's Ama Dablam," Dad said, pointing at a mountain off to the right. It's shorter than the really big ones, off on its own. It's a thumb of hard bare rock, with glaciers and ice below. Ama Dablam is the most beautiful mountain in the world, and it looks really hard to climb.

"What's Ama Dablam mean in Sherpa?" I asked Anu.

"Mother's Jewelry Box," Anu said. "See the ice there?"

He pointed at a glacier hanging on the mountain, below the summit, surrounded by rock and sparkling in the sun. "That's the jewelry box."

"They call Everest Chomolungma in Sherpa," Dad said. "It means Goddess Mother of the Snows."

We all looked at Everest again. Anu told me yesterday that Chomolungma means Mountain No Bird Can Fly Over. But Anu and me, we didn't say anything. Dad is the member.

Orrie

We finally got Andy away from Dead Yakky. "He'll be all right," Andy said.

It was only another hour's walk to the lodge where we were going to stay for the night. Other expeditions camp in tents all the way up. We stay in lodges, little hotels run by local people in old stone houses. Dad says it means we don't have to carry all that food and we get to meet people.

We got there in time for lunch. I had *momos*. They're like Tibetan ravioli. I had the ones with meat inside, to keep up my strength. After lunch we played with two kids about Andy's age who belonged to the house. Libby took out her sketchpad and started drawing pictures of the kids. The little boys watched with big eyes. Libby gave them pens and pages from her sketchbook. They drew page after page of helicopters, with little stick people leaning out of the helicopters.

Their mum told me the helicopters fly up here to rescue trekkers in trouble. The oldest boy wants to be a helicopter pilot when he grows up. Andy was drawing pictures of dead yaks.

After supper we all went to bed. I tucked Andy in. "Where did you learn all that stuff you said to Dead Yakky?"

"The monks in Namche," Andy said. "I asked them what they said to the dead people."

"They spoke English?"

"One of them did."

"How?"

"I don't know," Andy said. "Will Dead Yakky be all right?"

"Yes," I said. "You done good, kid. Sleep tight."

Andy lay there with his eyes closed, looking just like a normal nonweird kid. I went downstairs for a pee in the outside loo. I stood in the moonlight afterwards and watched Ama Dablam till I froze.

When I came back in the main door I heard people talking. It was Libby and the mum, sitting in the kitchen by the fire, talking like people whose work is done. Libby patted the bench next to her. She had a sleeping bag over her lap. She tucked the bag over me and put her arm round me. I don't like Libby, but I was cold. And I needed someone to put their arm round me.

"Do you like your husband climbing?" Libby said to the Sherpa mum.

"No," the mum said.

"I don't like it either," Libby said. She hugged me harder when she said that.

"I tell him he must stop," the mum said. "He says we need the money, to send the boys to good schools in Kathmandu. So they will not be poor, like us."

"And you do need the money," Libby said.

"I need him to be alive. What do I do with a dead husband? When he goes off on an expedition, we fight. I stand in the door and I put my arms around him to stop him leaving. He hits me so he can go."

"Don't let a man hit you," Libby said. She's so American.

"He does it so he can make money for the family," the mum said. "He is right."

"You're right, too," Libby said.

"I'm right, too," the woman said. "You want tea?" she asked me.

"No, thank you," I said, snuggling down under the sleeping bag. When you want to listen to grownups, you make yourself invisible and they'll say anything.

"Last year many expeditions were on Everest," the mum said. "My husband was there, too. Three Sherpas died on another expedition. They were all from the village of Phortse, across the valley. The Sherpa sardar of the expedition, he is a good man. He walked to Phortse to tell the wives their men had died. But when he got there he could not speak. He was so ashamed. The women of Phortse knew from his face that someone had died, but they did not know who."

Dad wasn't here. He must have gone to bed without Libby. Why?

"Wasn't there a rescue team?" Libby said.

"No," she said. "They died in avalanche. No one could get to them. And the helicopters cannot go that high for anyone."

"Oh," Libby said.

"At Phortse the sardar sat there, silent. The women of Phortse ran down to the river and up to Tangboche monastery to ask the monks who had died. The monks told them. The three wives of the dead men shouted. I heard their shouts from here."

The monastery must be a mile away from here as the crow flies, but many hours' walk down to the river and up to Tangboche. They must have been really screaming.

"I thought, my husband is on Everest. I must stop him.

I wrote him a letter. I said I was very sick, the doctor in Kunde says maybe I will die, I have to take the helicopter to hospital in Kathmandu. Then I gave the letter to a boy to take to my husband on Everest. My husband was just putting his boots on at Base Camp to go into the icefall and up the mountain when the boy got there. He read the letter and ran straight down to me. That usually takes three days. He did it in five hours."

I could tell how proud she was of her strong husband, and of his fear for her.

"He came here," the mum said. "He looked at me." Her eyes went wide, to show his surprise.

"And there was nothing wrong with you," Libby said.

"Yes. He was very angry. He said, this is my job, you have ruined my job. I was so afraid for you, he shouts. I said to him, now you know how I feel. Every time you leave."

Libby laughed, a big laugh from the belly. The mum laughed with her, so I did, too.

"He stopped being angry, just like that," the woman said. "He understood. He loves me."

"A good man," Libby said.

"A good man," the mum said. "That is why I want him alive. Then he went back to climb Everest."

The flames of the fire danced in the cold. The Sherpa mum had big brass plates on the wall and enormous copper bowls on the shelves. The orange and red of the flames flickered on the bowls. I went to sleep with Libby's arm round me.

It doesn't mean anything.

Jack

We've been walking up from Namche for three days. The air is getting tight up here. I can see Anu looking at me, worrying. There's nothing to worry about.

The porters for other expeditions carry enormous loads. Some of them are just children. I caught up with one girl just before Dole, at the top of a long climb through trees covered in hanging moss. She was six inches shorter than me and was carrying a cardboard box twice her size. The box was tied to a basket on her shoulders.

She stopped and rested her load on a boulder. I rested my pack on the next boulder. I asked her with hand signals if I could try to carry her load. She smiled. She had a jewel in her nose, and the cute tipped-up eyelids Sherpa girls have. All she had on her feet were plastic sandals. She slipped her basket off her shoulders. I took her place and put the carrying ropes round my shoulders. We laughed shyly as we moved round each other.

I braced my legs and stood up. Pain raced up my back and pushed the air out of my lungs. I put the basket back down on the boulder.

The girl was giggling at me, her hand over her mouth. I

think she was maybe thirteen, about my age. Sherpas are shorter than us. It was sort of OK she was laughing at me, because I could tell she liked me.

But I didn't know what to do. So I said like, "Later, I'll be seeing you," or something that stupid, in English. And I gave a little wave and walked on.

I probably would have said something stupid even if I'd been able to talk Sherpa. Maybe she thought I was saying something cool because she couldn't understand it. I looked back and she gave a little wave, just like mine.

I bet they pay her three cents a day to carry that load.

That night we slept at Machermo. Anu told me that a Sherpa girl was attacked by a yeti in Machermo a few years ago. A yeti is something that lives in the high snows, half man and half animal. In English he's called the abominable snowman and seems like a monster. To Anu it's another one of the dangers of the mountains, like bears and avalanches. He says yetis even kill yaks. They jump on them and go for the neck. But the yeti didn't kill the girl in Machermo, it just left a big wound down the side of her head. That's how they know it was a yeti, because she lived to tell them.

The next day we walked up the gorge to Gokyo. We were up just before dawn. The sky was gray. It had snowed in the night. The land in front of us was smooth and white.

Anu led the way, making footprints a foot deep. It was hard for Andy. The footprints were too far apart for him. He kept walking beside them and falling through the snow. Anu came back and said he'd carry Andy. Andy said no, but Anu carried him anyway. He and Dad took turns. Cookie Wolf is so light he just raced back and forth across the snow.

We went down along a hillside and crossed the river where it came tumbling down from the glacier. There was a little wooden bridge of logs laid together, with ice on them. I took off my gloves and used my stick for balance. On the other side I turned and looked back at where we'd come from. Our footsteps cut through the smoothness of the snow, saying men had been here.

Then we were up to the valley of Gokyo. The glacier runs down the middle of the valley, one of the longest glaciers in Asia. The sides of the glacier come up high. Beyond the sides, against the mountains, was the narrow Gokyo Valley itself. The river ran through it, making lakes. The first lake we came to was a frozen pond. The second lake was bigger, covered in a sheet of ice with a dusting of new snow on top. One far corner of the lake was open water, a startling glacial blue against the white of the snow. A family of ducks paddled in the water, their feathers blue and red. How they live in this cold I do not know.

The lake made a constant groaning sound, like a giant in pain. Dad said it was the ice expanding and getting ready to split as the day warmed up.

It was flatter, and Andy could walk on his own here. There were cairns every few feet along the path, flat rocks piled on top of each other by men who had been this way before. They looked like stone guardians in the wilderness. The clouds were lifting. The blue of the lake was deep. Suddenly the ice on the lake cracked like thunder.

We were all going slowly now, stopping to breathe. It wasn't just me. Gokyo is over sixteen thousand feet, as high as the summit of Mont Blanc, the highest peak in the Alps.

We met a party of porters trudging down from the glacier. Some were wearing thin canvas shoes. One was wearing plastic shoes, in the snow. Dad and Anu and me stopped to talk to their sardar, because they'd just been climbing Island Peak. We still haven't seen it. The sardar was a big man for a Sherpa, chunky across the shoulders. But he was only carrying a little day pack, like a school book bag, because he was the sardar.

Dad asked the sardar how Island Peak was.

"Lots of snow," the sardar said. "And crevasses." A crevasse is a hole in the ice. On a big mountain like Island Peak, the snow falls and crushes the old snow beneath into thick layers of ice. So great sheets of ice move very slowly down the mountain, like a silent frozen river, a few inches a day. The ice can be three hundred feet thick. As it moves over the uneven rock below, the ice bends and breaks. Holes open up, cracks and canyons in the ice. The snow lies on top of these crevasses. And you don't see them till you fall through the snow.

"Bad crevasses?" Dad asked the sardar.

"Bad. But not too bad," the sardar said.

"Did you make it?" Dad asked.

"All members make the summit."

Another porter passed. His feet were wet and he was staggering under a big bag.

"How much do they carry?" I asked the sardar.

"Thirty kilos," the sardar said, like he was offended. "All my men carry thirty kilos up here. Other expeditions make them carry fifty, sixty kilos. Not me." Sixty kilos is 132 pounds. These are small men. A lot of them are my size. No wonder Dad wants us to carry our own gear up to Island Peak.

The third lake was bigger. At the head of it was the village of Gokyo, with some huts and four small stone lodges. This used to be summer pastures for the yaks, and in winter no one ever lived up here. But that was before the trekkers came.

We stayed in the poshest lodge. The bunk beds in the

61

dormitory were made out of solid varnished pine. Somebody must have carried those pine logs up here. I bagged one of the bottom bunks. Usually I sleep on the top bunk, but this time I was so tired I was afraid I'd fall trying to get out of bed for a pee in the night.

I lay on my bed and just breathed for hours.

They called me into the other room for supper. Dad said we were all going to climb Gokyo Ri, the hill above Gokyo, tomorrow morning. That way we could look at Island Peak and see how to climb it. Orrie said she needed a day's rest before she did anything. She looked at me with her face full of meaning. Like I should say I needed a day's rest, too.

Sure. Then Dad wouldn't let me climb Island Peak.

Orrie

Jack never listens to anything I say anymore.

He just pecked at his food. I had a big pancake with butter, and another, and then another. You burn up so many calories just shivering up here, you can eat like a vacuum cleaner and still look like a model.

Libby and Dad are fighting. I'm sure of it now. They're all nice to each other when we're around, consulting what each one wants, trying to show themselves and us how much they love each other. That's one sign. People who really love each other just get on with their lives. And there's like this tense shimmering force field in the air between them. You can't miss it when grownups are in trouble.

The way to stay happy is not to want other people.

Climbing gives you good leg muscles, too. Not that anybody sees your legs up here. It's too cold. I wonder if Sherpas take their clothes off to make babies. I wonder if they even take their clothes off to have babies.

Andy didn't want to leave Cookie Wolf outside in the snow. So I sneaked the dog into the dormitory under my coat and he got into Andy's sleeping bag. I left them, their two little noses poking out of the hood of the sleeping bag together.

Libby isn't going up to Gokyo Ri either.

I don't want Dad to be with Libby. But if Libby and Dad split up, I'm going to be throwing up in wastebaskets again, like I did when Dad left us.

I'm worried about Jack.

Jack

Dad woke me up two hours before dawn so we could be on the summit of Gokyo Ri in time to see the sunrise over Everest. He put a hand on my cheek and waited for me to wake up. I couldn't see him in the dark but I knew he was smiling.

I made myself get out of my sleeping bag. I've come to love my sleeping bag. You know how when you have a favorite shirt or pair of trainers and it's been through a lot with you? I'm starting to feel that way about my sleeping bag. If I'm not careful, I'm going to give it a pet name, like Tigger or Snuggles.

Charles Cresswell in my class has given his willie a pet name. I'm the only one who knows.

My head hurt. I pulled my boots on in the dark. Something licked my hand. I almost yelled. It was Cookie Wolf.

When I got to the door the stars hit me. The clouds had gone and the sky was full of points of light like needles. Dad had a big hot thermos full of tea with lashings of sugar. That's really good when you're so cold your willie's shriveled. Charles Cresswell calls his Smoothie. He thinks that's cool. Charles has a long, difficult road ahead of him.

Orrie worries that sugar in her tea will make her fat. I don't. I'm a naturally fit person. Sometimes when no one else is home I stand in front of the mirror naked and slap my stomach just to show how hard it is.

I'm thinking of calling my willie Everest.

Anu was with us. I don't think he's going to let any of us go off on our own. We got the tea down, sipping as fast as we could, but it was really hot. We were wearing torches on our heads, like miners' lamps.

We started off across the snow, Dad first, then me, then Anu. The surface of the snow had frozen hard in the night, almost like ice. All we could see in the dark was the bulk of Gokyo Ri curving up like the back of a whale. Partway up the hill were the lights of a party that had started ahead of us, bobbing along. They looked like a bunch of wee Smurfs going off to work.

We started up the hill. Slog, slog, slog. Dad went ahead. Then he caught himself and sat on a boulder, waiting for me and Anu.

"You OK, Jack?" he said.

"Yes." I breathed some more, to get more air to speak. "I'm fine."

"You don't have to do this, you know."

"I'm fine." I do have to do this.

He peered at me, like you can tell from a person's face if they're lying. That works with Andy. It doesn't work with me. You learn how to control your face as you grow up.

I charged past him. He had to get up and follow me.

I pushed down hard on the snow with each step. Some people give up in life. Then the world walks on their faces and they whine about how unfair it is. You walk on the world or they walk on you. That's what I've seen. It's not fair. The people who get walked on, they're the good people. But I don't want to be one of them. I don't want my children to have a weak father.

65

The mountain went on and on. Dad just kept pace behind me. I know he's watching me. There are days at school, standing there in the playground, wishing I knew how to talk to girls, when all I want to do is scream. And keep screaming. I can talk to Orrie all right. She's not a girl, she's just a human. I can ask her anything. She says all girls are human. She says I should just talk to them like they're human and they'll talk back. This is not a realistic attitude. I can't talk to Orrie anymore anyway.

The sky was growing lighter and the wash of stars was leaving us. Only the few brightest stars were still shining. Plod, plod.

Charles Cresswell is my best friend. He's a nerd, too. He understands, and he forgives. But he couldn't do this.

We were there. The summit of Gokyo Ri. There was a jumble of rocks. Ropes with lines of prayer flags were strung between the rocks. We sat on a flat boulder taller than a man and looked at the mountains. I've never felt such happiness. Joy coming up from the mountain, through my feet, spilling through my chest, making my face red with happiness.

People are so hard, and mountains are so easy.

The sun came up over Everest. Each mountain is different in its shape and its feel. You learn them like you learn boats, or the faces of people you love. Most of the mountains up here are beautiful. The hanging glaciers, the flutings of ice that fall from the ridges. And each one has a different Sherpa god.

But Everest is ugly. The others are white with ice. Everest is black rock. There are no curves in it. The mountain is a pyramid. I could see two sides, slabs of hard rock, the line of the West Ridge dividing them. It's black because it's so steep the snow won't stick. Some mountains can be your friends, like Cho Oyu at the head of the Gokyo Valley. Some are beautiful, like Tamserku. But Everest is just strength, defiant. It looks like a place that kills men on purpose.

I'm going to climb it one day.

And there in front of Everest was Island Peak, our mountain. It's only 1,500 feet higher than Gokyo Ri. I can do it. But the ri is a hill. Island is a Himalayan peak. It's a pure white wall of snow, wide and steep. Beyond and above that, where we can't see, is the summit plateau. The first day you climb most of the steep side. The second day you clump across the long summit plateau that rises slowly to the summit at the far end. Then you hurry down.

Anu traced the route for us. About halfway up the first day's climb are the black rocks, sticking out of the snow. You clamber across them, keeping low, and back onto the wall. Then you walk up at an angle to the right.

It looks terribly steep. But all the mountains up here look steeper from a distance than they do once you're on them. I hope.

I looked at Island Peak and began to love it.

Dad got out three chocolate bars. He always has chocolate bars whenever we climb a hill in Scotland. It's his way of saying I love you. When he used to fight with Mum, afterwards Dad would go out to Safeways and come back with chocolate ice cream for the whole family. We'd eat maybe three tubs together and all feel better.

I crunched the chocolate bar. It was frozen hard and made my teeth skitter.

The sun was up now. It turned the snow on the wall of Island Peak to a soft reddish orange. Like the most beautiful sunset I've ever seen. But it was dawn in the Himalayas, and it wasn't the sky changing colors. It was the earth.

All around us there were trekkers, the ones who had set out earlier and the ones who had come after us. Every one of them pulled a camera out as they got to the summit. They took pictures for an hour or so. When they were finished, they put the cameras back in their fanny packs and started down the mountain. Not once did one of them look at anything without a camera on his face. They saw nothing. If God appeared to them, they'd take His picture.

Anu saw one of his Sherpa friends with the photographers and went over to talk to him.

"Happy?" Dad said.

"Yes," I said.

"I love it here. I wanted you to see it. On the subway in New York, I close my eyes and see Gokyo."

"Thanks, Dad."

I loved Gokyo Ri then. I'll come back up here lots of times. And when I'm old and Dad's dead, I'll come back up here and pray for him.

"Don't you like New York?" I said.

"I hate my job," Dad said.

I didn't know that. "Why?"

"I lie. I write advertising copy for medicines. For doctors to read who are too busy to read articles in medical journals. 'Your patient has a desperate fear of loneliness? Shut her up by stuffing her full of Panthrax pills.' That's what I write."

"Why do you do it?"

"I need the money."

"You and Libby have enough money," I said. Compared to Mum and us, they have a lot of money.

"It costs a lot to live in New York," Dad said, "and I send a lot to your mother."

"Don't do it if you hate it, Dad. Not for us."

"We need the money." He was on the edge of anger. I know. He used to get angry a lot when he lived with us. I shut up. The funny thing is, I knew he wasn't telling the

69

truth about why he did his job. He had that tinny sound in his voice grownups have when they think they're telling the truth but really they're not. We sat and ate chocolate for a while.

"Have you thought about living with us in New York?" Dad asked. His voice was almost begging.

"Yes."

"And?"

"I don't know."

"I just want you to know that we love you," Dad said, "and we always have a place for you."

I think Dad needs me to come and live with him really badly. It's like he's lonely, even though he has Libby. Like if we come to live with him, then he wasn't wrong to leave Mum.

I want to go live with Dad. I want to be a man who climbs mountains, not the silly housework boy who cleans up after a crazy mother. I hate my mum for that. But she needs me.

"Have you talked with Orrie?" Dad asked.

"Yes." I couldn't say we're not really talking about anything. "She doesn't know what she wants." I'm pretty sure that's true.

"Do you know what you want?"

"I want to come live with you," I said.

I don't really know what I want. But now he has to let me climb Island Peak.

Orrie

We made it. We're at Island Peak Base Camp. It was two days' hard walking, across the Gokyo Glacier and then up to Base Camp. It's a beautiful day, clear and windless. Base Camp is a small, flat, rocky place on the edge of where the snow begins. Two hundred feet from us, Island Peak seems to go straight up.

We've got two tents here now. We're all scrunched together, so we didn't have to carry so much. The grownups are in the blue tent, the kids in the orange one. Tomorrow Dad and Anu and Jack are taking the blue one up to the peak. Me and Libby and Andy are staying down here because we're girls.

That's what they think.

Jack

I went straight to sleep when we got to camp. I kept waking up, the same dream over and over again.

It was about the girl who let me try to lift her basket. She was sitting alone at a fire she'd made in one of the little stone huts the yak herders build. Those huts are maybe four feet high, with room for two people sitting together. They shelter you from the rain, but there's no door —

they're open. She was crouched on her haunches, her hands up to the fire, thinking of the weak white boy with the nice smile who couldn't lift her load. Suddenly the hut was full, an animal bigger than a man, its shaggy fur all matted and orange. The smell of blood and fear came off the animal in waves. A yeti. She stuck her hand in the flames and grabbed a burning stick. The animal filled the whole hut, his jaw only inches from her, his body all around her. She shoved the red hot wood into his face. His claws shot out and scraped down her head and body, and the yeti was gone screaming into the night.

She knew she'd have to wait huddled in the hut until dawn. She couldn't go into the dark with the smell of her own blood on her. There was snuffling and whimpering outside the hut. Something made a sort of chortling call, begging her to come out away from the fire and play. The pain of the cuts ate into her head. She ran out of wood.

I woke up. And lay there, the pain drilling into my head. And went back to sleep, and dreamed the dream again. And woke, the pain filling my head.

Orrie

Jack's been hyper the last two days. Something's wrong with him. Even though I can see the tiredness all over his body, his eyes are wild and burning. He really wants to climb Island Peak.

The way I know something is wrong is it's me who's looking after Andy. The last two days of walking, it's been Libby or me with Andy every step of the way. And Cookie Wolf, of course. He never leaves Andy's side.

Usually Jack would be looking after Andy. That's what Jack does. He looks after people. Now he's just looking after himself. I think it's because there's nothing left over for anybody else. I'm worried about him.

Way high above us I saw an eagle drifting in the wind. Only Dad said it was a vulture. I went and asked Anu. He was cooking a stew for all of us. It smelled like heaven.

"What is the difference?" Anu said.

"Vultures eat dead animals," I said. "Eagles fly down out of the sky and grab animals." I flapped my arms like great outstretched wings and curved my fingers into talons.

"That bird up there eats dead animals," Anu said. "Look at the head. Very small."

I craned my neck. The bird seemed to float, thousands of feet above us. It must have been eight feet from wingtip to wingtip. But its head was small and hooked and weird looking. A vulture.

"They eat people, too," Anu said.

"People?"

"We Sherpas burn our dead. Tibetan people, they leave the dead people out for that bird. It comes and eats them.

When I was a boy, our neighbors were Tibetans. They came over the pass when the Chinese invaded Tibet. The old mother died and they took her up to the mountain and chopped her up with big knives. My family went too, to be nice; we were neighbors. And then we waited. Hours. Those big birds here in Sherpa country, they don't know about Tibetan funerals. Finally it was almost dark and one bird came down and started eating. I watched everything. I was a boy."

"Will the vulture eat us?"

"We won't die," Anu said.

"No?"

"No. It is my job. No one will die."

"Should Jack be climbing tomorrow?" I asked.

Anu looked away from me.

"Anu," I said, real fierce.

"Your father says what happens."

Jack's sick. Anu knows it.

I went to our tent and unzipped the door. Jack was lying in his sleeping bag, his eyes open, staring at nothing.

"How's it going, bro?"

"It's going," he said.

"You OK?"

"Yes."

"Really?" I asked.

"Yes."

I sat down by his head and put my hand on his forehead to check his temperature. He jerked his head away. I reached out with the other hand and grabbed his face and held it so I could check his temperature.

"You're hot."

"Your hands are freezing," Jack said. "You've been outside."

Probably true. Maybe true. "You shouldn't climb tomorrow," I said.

"You're just jealous."

"Not," I said.

"You think Dad loves me more than he does you."

I don't think that. I know it. Dad's always loved Jack more. It's because he's a boy. "No I don't," I said.

"He doesn't," Jack said. "I don't know how much he really loves anyone."

"He's fighting with Libby," I said.

"I know," Jack said.

"Do you know what they're fighting about?"

"No." His face crumpled. "I hate it when they fight."

"Yes."

We both thought about that.

"I'm going to tell Dad you're too sick to climb tomorrow."

He grabbed my wrist. "Don't do that," he said.

"I have to, Jack. I don't want you to die."

"Anu won't let me go up if I'm too sick."

"Anu's just doing what Dad tells him to."

"If you make Dad stop me climbing the mountain," Jack said, "I'll go live with Dad and leave you alone with Andy and Mum."

I ran out of the tent.

Jack

I didn't mean it. I wouldn't do that. I just had to stop her. If I climb the mountain, Dad will love me properly.

I'm so tired.

Orrie

I don't know what to do. If I tell on Jack, he'll never forgive me.

Jack's the rock of my life.

I hate Anu for being too weak to stand up to Dad. I hate Dad for not seeing what's happening. I hate myself for not telling Dad.

Who am I kidding? Dad wouldn't listen to me anyway.

Jack

Anu woke us all up while it was still dark. I lurched around the tent, stuffing last-minute things into my rucksack, while a half-awake Orrie muttered filthy words. Cookie Wolf tried to get into my rucksack.

I got out of the tent. The wall of Island Peak rose in front of us, a phantom gray in the starlight, seeming to go up forever.

Orrie came out and hugged me goodbye. "Give 'em hell, tiger," she said. Then she put her lips to my ear and said, "Be careful. I love you."

"I will," I said.

Andy gave me a little blue stone with shiny bits of quartz in it. Because it was still dark, I had my headlamp switched on and the quartz twinkled in the light. "It's my magic stone," Andy said. "Leave it on the summit."

"I will," I said.

"Cookie Wolf says he wants to come with you," Andy said. "But I told him he was too little and his head might explode from the altitude."

"Good thinking," I said.

"Cookie Wolf wants you to kiss him goodbye."

I did. It turned out Cookie Wolf did want that.

"You OK?" Libby asked me.

"I'm OK."

"Would you lie to me?"

"No."

Dad came up to give Libby a kiss. She turned her face

away and he hugged her. They didn't say anything.

Dad turned and started up the mountain. Anu and I followed.

We got to the bottom of the wall and started up. Dad took the lead. He leaned forward into the wind. Making the footsteps — breaking the trail — is the hardest part, because it takes so much energy to keep breaking through the snow.

I followed Dad, putting my feet in each of his deep footsteps. It was walking, not climbing with ropes and your hands, but it was steep and hard.

I was wearing crampons for the first time. Anu showed me how to put them on. Each crampon fits over a boot. The sole of the crampon is made up of pointed metal teeth that dig into the ice and stop you from slipping.

I've got an ice ax, too. It's about three feet high and shaped like a T. The bottom of the T is a pointed metal bit you stick into the snow to use like a walking stick. It helps me keep my balance. One end of the top of the T is a pointed ax for hacking at ice. The other end is a broad blade, a bit like a hoe. When you start to fall on ice or snow, you smash the hoe end into the snow above your head and it slows you down, dragging like an anchor. Anu's been showing me how to do that.

I have goggles too, tinted to protect against snow blindness. Dad bought ski goggles to fit me in Namche, but brought welders' goggles from home for himself. He says they're half the price. And they're the real thing. Men use them to work.

And I have my lamp, with its little battery, shining on my forehead. There's a red headband that holds it on, and I carry a spare battery in my rucksack.

I've got everything, really.

The mountain went up and up in the darkness. Now only the brightest stars shone on. In the dawn I saw something with all the colors of the rainbow. But it was far broader than a rainbow and went straight up from the ground. The colored light seemed to bend and ripple in the air.

"Look behind you," Dad shouted, and I did. There was another straight rainbow coming up from the ground at the opposite end of the mountain wall.

I looked back and forth. I expected the two pillars of light to come together above me, but they didn't. I had never heard of this, had no name for it. I asked Dad what it was.

"Don't know," he said, his voice full of wonder.

"I have never seen it," Anu said.

I watched, afraid at every moment that this new thing would disappear. And then, after five minutes or thirty, I have no way of telling, it went.

Anu took over the lead from Dad. I was still second,

between them, with Dad taking up the rear like a sheep-dog. My feet were heavy, like I had weights tied to them. They ached the way they do when I have a fever and get to stay home from school. The cold air hurt my sore throat every time I breathed. I felt like there was something across my chest, some cruel strap constantly being pulled tighter. But I didn't care. I was climbing. The Himalayas. The top of the world.

Orrie

Dad's not doing this to me.

After dawn Libby, Andy, and me sat around watching the others climb. Dad and Anu were little red dots. Jack was a purple dot. He loves that purple down jacket. It's so big and puffy he looks little inside it, but he thinks it makes him look big.

Libby said she was fed up with watching the big boys play. I suggested she take Andy down the valley to play around the river. Andy loves that. They'll be gone for hours.

Jack

We stopped and took off our crampons when we got to the rocks. I needed a rest badly. So did Dad.

I looked down. The orange tent was tiny, far below. The slope hadn't been too bad when we were climbing. But when I looked down now, it seemed to drop away like a cliff.

Dad got three chocolate bars out of his bag, one for each of us.

"Peace, ay?" Dad said.

"Peace."

"I wanted you to see this."

"Thanks, Dad."

"It doesn't have to be like it is down there."

We looked down the valley. The clouds were starting to move up the Gokyo Valley, the way they do every day. They were starting earlier today, though, and were darker.

"I do not like those clouds," Anu said.

"They're all right," Dad said.

"They do not look good."

"They're all right!" Dad shouted.

A shake went right through the whole of Anu's body.

"I'm sorry," Dad said to Anu.

"Whatever you say," Anu said.

We finished our chocolate bars and put our packs back on. We scrambled across the rocks. We didn't say anything, but I think we were all going as fast as we could to get as far as possible before the clouds caught us.

Orrie

Jack and the others got to the rocks on the ridge and went

round the corner. I couldn't see them and they couldn't see me. I left a note for Libby on her pillow and went off, up the mountain.

I've got crampons. I whined at Dad in Namche until he rented a pair for me. I've got an ice ax, too. They're moving really slowly. By the time I catch up with them they won't be able to turn back.

I don't take crap.

Jack

Foot. In. Foot. In. Foot. In. Keep moving. Breathe. Foot. Breathe. Foot. Breathe. Never say die.

I looked back down. We were round the corner of the rocks. I couldn't see the tent. The clouds were coming up the hill at us.

Orrie

The first bit was easy. Like when they let you out of school on the last day before summer and you're running down the road with your mates, screaming and swinging round lampposts.

It got hard following in their tracks. The steps were too far apart and their boots made deep holes in the snow. I had to yank one foot out for each step, bend my knee up almost to a high kick, and then plop it in the next hole.

I was singing "The Battle Hymn of the Republic"— Mine eyes have seen the glory of the coming of the Lord, He is trampling out the vintage where the grapes of wrath are stored—and having a whale of a time. But then I thought maybe someone would think I was yelling for help. Sound travels a long way in the thin air up here. So I shut up.

I looked back down and the clouds were moving up the Gokyo Valley the way they do every day.

I moved out of the footsteps. They were too much like hard work. I'm little and light — I don't sink so far into the snow. It's hard making my own steps, too, but it's easier than playing giant steps with boys. I'm going faster now.

I see one of Anu's big vultures way above me. He just hangs and floats there. He never seems to dive for food. It's like he can see a hundred miles in every direction, and in all that space there's not one dead rabbit. Maybe it's because there's so few living things up here. This is like a desert, because all the water is frozen.

I wonder where the vultures nest.

Two

The Climb

Jack

The clouds are upon us. We've taken off our packs. Anu is setting up the tent. He's not saying anything.

"You OK?" Dad asks Anu.

"Ump."

"Good," he says. But he's looking at me. It's strange seeing his face with dark goggles on, like he's not really there. I don't know why we're still wearing goggles. It's gray-white all around us and you can't see ten yards in the snow.

I take my goggles off so I can see better. Dad's still looking at me with his goggle eyes like an alien. He's got white beard stubble coming in round the goggles. He takes them off and looks straight at me. His eyes are brown. They bore into mine, asking a question.

I look back into his eyes. You can look into the eyes and see the whole person inside, alive behind there. Eyes can't move and make expressions like the face. They don't have any surface. I don't know why you can see everything in them.

He still doesn't speak, and I look right back. I try to make my eyes tough and hard. So he won't see how sick I am, how afraid. But if I can see straight into him, then he can see right into me.

He's afraid, and now he's angry. I'm afraid of my father's anger. I always have been. He yelled when I was little. A lot. With his hands flying over his head in rage, like a man fighting off bats only he could see. He never hit us. He didn't hit children. I think he didn't dare.

His eyes are really angry now, showing the red inside his brain. Because I'm sick. Because we're going to have to turn around because of me. Because he hasn't paid any attention to what's wrong with me. Because he didn't listen to Anu. Because he hates himself. We never say anything about my father's anger outside the family. And the funny thing is he never hurts us. But I'm scared of the shouting.

I wish he'd say something. I don't have anything to say. I'll stare Dad down if I have to this time. I don't really know why he's angry. I'm just guessing. All my life I've guessed, to stop the anger from happening.

"Jack." He makes his voice gentle, reaches his arms out. But I can hear the rage underneath making his voice shake.

"Jack." I'm staring straight back. I've always looked away. We all always looked away. The hardest thing is waiting all the time for the anger. Never knowing when it's going to come. Being real careful, watching. Trying to please him. Because I want him to love me.

I think that's what drove Mum crazy.

His hands are on my shoulders, and he's shaking me. His gloves hurt my shoulders. He's grabbed me to him, and he's hugging me, crushing me. He says, "Jack, it's going to be all right. You'll be all right, Jack. We'll all be all right." And I know he loves me.

The wind is beginning to howl around us. The air is full of snow. I bury my head in Dad's chest and put my arms around him. They don't meet around his back. He's a big man.

Anu is saying something to Dad. I can't hear what it is. I'm all muffled into Dad's down jacket. There's a picture of him and me in Mum's album at home. I'm a newborn baby. We're lying in bed, him and me both naked, but there's covers over most of us. You can see his broad chest and his face, and he's looking at me with such love. I'm smiling a stupid happy baby smile back at him. Mum took the picture.

Dad lets go of me and listens to Anu. I still can't make out what they're saying. They move off.

Anu's hacking at the snow with the blade of his ice ax. Dad gets down on his hands and knees and starts shoveling away the snow that Anu has loosened. Like a dog digging. After a while Anu stops and leans on his ice ax to breathe. Dad takes the ax and they change places.

Dad's taking care of us.

They take turns. I sit down in the snow and watch. I ought to be helping them, but I can't. They don't ask me to.

They're digging out a platform for the tent. That's what they're doing. So the wind doesn't blow us away down the mountain. They're digging into the side of the mountain, making a flat step in all the steepness. A little home.

They're taking care of me. I've got to stay awake until I can get into that tent.

I'm cold.

Orrie

When I reach the rocks, I lose Dad and Jack's trail. I sit down and take off my crampons. They're worse than useless on rock. But it takes forever to get them off. My fingers are too cold to undo the knots. At least my fingers still hurt. When you can't feel the pain, that's frostbite.

It's snowing. The air is gray with snowflakes. The wind is

so strong the snow can't fall—it just blows straight into my face. The snowflakes sting like needles.

It's getting not so good here. I better catch up with Dad and Jack. I've been going a lot faster than them. I'm little, but I'm faster. Like Cookie Wolf.

The rocks are big curved boulders, fallen on top of each other, each resting on the ones below. I test each one. If it isn't anchored, it will go and take me with it. It's not falling I'm afraid of. It's breaking an ankle. If I can't walk, I'm in trouble. Dead Yakky kind of trouble.

It's getting harder to see. I know the boys were going to cut across the rocks and get back to the snow on the other side. I take what's obviously the easiest route. I think I see some marks of their passing in the snow. They must have gone this way.

I'm across the rocks, back on the edge of the snow. I can't see any tracks. Dad and Jack didn't come here. I got it wrong. I start whooping. Breathing out too fast, afraid.

Hold my breath. Think fluffy bunnies. Calm. Think Andy. Think sweet song. Breathe.

I'm OK. Think.

I'm at the edge of the rocks. They either went above here or below here. They can't be far off. I haven't come very far across the rocks. All I have to do is scramble down the edge of the rocks. If the tracks are there, I'm OK. If not, I'll come back up and look above here. Either way, I'll find them.

I'm moving fast now, going down, from boulder to boulder. A rock twists under my foot. I leap and land on another boulder, spread-eagled, my hands and feet clutching the rock. My knee hurts like crazy. I get up. I'm OK. I can walk.
   Careful. Slower.
   I pull my glove off and look at my watch. It's four o'clock. I've been climbing down for half an hour. I haven't found anything. They must have gone across farther up. I turn back up and begin to climb. It's safer than going down. My body just keeps moving up. Any trouble and I just grab the rock above me and move fast. But it's hard work.

It's ten past five. I'm way above where I started. Nothing. It's nearly dark with the snow. It'll be night soon. I sit down and eat three of the four chocolate bars I brought up to share with the others. I'm saving the last for later.
   I start screaming for help.

Jack

In the tent between Dad and Anu, each time I go to sleep I dream I'm drowning. And wake up afraid.
   I dream again. I'm going under, screaming for help.

92

Orrie's screaming, too. I wake up. I hear Orrie screaming in the wind. It's faint, hard to hear under the noise of the wind rattling the tent. But it's her.

"Orrie!" I shout.

"It's OK," Dad says.

"Orrie." I have no breath.

"It's OK, son."

"He's sick," Anu says.

I can't talk. I have no air.

"It was a bad dream," Dad says to me. "That's all."

"He has altitude sickness," Anu says. He rolls over in his sleeping bag. His face is inches from mine. "We must take him down the mountain."

I pull all the air into my lungs and say, "Dad! Listen for Orrie."

"Orrie?"

"She's out there. I can hear her."

We three lie together, listening to the wind.

"She's —" Dad starts, and I shut him up by saying, "Listen!"

They listen some more. *I* can't hear her now either.

"Orrie's safe," Dad says. "She's down at Base Camp, snug as a bug in a rug. Drinking tea and reading Andy a story."

"Give me your hand," Anu says.

My hands are warm down inside my sleeping bag. I'm not

going to let them get outside in the cold. Anu unzips my sleeping bag. The cold rushes in. I kick out and try to get away. The light from Anu's headlamp flashes round the tent as he tries to catch my hand. Anu takes off my glove and holds my hand. It feels good for someone to hold my hand.

"See the fingernails?" Anu says.

"Yes," Dad says. He hovers over me, propped on one arm.

"Blue," Anu says. "Altitude sickness."

Orrie is out there, drowning in the wind, and the grownups are talking garbage.

"Hold your finger out," Dad says. I don't understand.

Dad lifts me so I'm sitting up. He pulls my arm out so it's hanging in the air, far away. He's holding my hand. I like that. He doesn't hold my hand as much as he used to.

"Touch your nose," Dad says.

I pull my arm back. My finger goes plonk on my cheek.

Dad takes my hand and pulls my arm out straight again. He shines his headlamp on my finger. "Look at your finger, Jack," he says. "Concentrate. Then touch your nose with it."

I sit up straight and stare at my finger. I bring it to my face, real slow and careful. I poke the middle of my forehead. I giggle till I can't breathe. I fall over sideways.

"We go down now," Anu says.

"It's a hurricane out there," Dad says.

"We wait for morning, your child dies," Anu says.

My head is in Dad's lap. His hands are stroking my hair. "OK," he says. "We'll go."

I'm sick. That's good. It wasn't Orrie out there. I imagined it.

Orrie

No one heard me.

If I fall asleep I won't wake up.

I can't feel my fingers and toes.

Jack

Anu and Dad are moving round the tent, packing. There's not enough room.

"Take the sleeping bags," Anu says. "Leave the rest."

"The tent cost money," Dad says. He flaps his hand.

"Maybe we have to carry him," Anu says.

"You can't carry me," I say. "I'm big."

"You can carry a man when you have to," Anu says. He's talking to Dad, not me.

I'm not going to climb the mountain after all. Everyone will laugh at me.

They're pulling me out of my sleeping bag. Dad puts my boots on, tying my crampons. Anu buttons up my coat. I feel like a little kid getting ready to play in the snow.

Anu is mumbling to himself. I can hear Dad whispering,

"Jesus, please. Jesus, please. Jesus, please." Anu must be praying to Buddha.

"You won't get to climb the mountain," I say to Dad. "I'm sorry."

"It doesn't matter," he says. "It really, really doesn't matter."

I'm dressed. We crawl out of the tent. The noise of the wind fills the world. No way could I have heard Orrie. It's completely dark. I stand. The wind knocks me over.

Dad puts his arms around my chest and hauls me up. We're standing. He's holding me. "I'm sorry, Dad," I say. We're all going to die because I wanted to climb the mountain.

"Don't be sorry, Jack," Dad says. "Live. Just walk." We start walking. Anu goes in front, stepping in the footsteps we made coming up. I follow him. Dad is behind me. Each time I fall over, Dad picks me up. I'm not afraid anymore. I'm kind of floating. It doesn't hurt when I fall over.

"Come on, Jack," Dad shouts. The snow hurts when it hits my eyes. I want to close my eyes. But I need them open to walk. Dad's turned on the light on my forehead, so I can see the steps.

We've been walking a long time. Dad's behind me, saying with every step, "Keep going, Jack. You can do it. You can do it." I can hear he's afraid for me. I fall over again. Dad picks me up, pulling my left arm tight to him so he can hold me up. My legs are sort of sloppy every which way. They don't do what I tell them. Dad's dragging me.

Anu stops. We stop, too.

"The road is gone," Anu says.

"What?" Dad yells against the wind.

"Look," Anu says. He takes off his headlamp and shines it along the snow ahead of us. "Our footsteps are gone," he says. The new snow has filled up our trail. We don't know where we are.

"What do we do?" Dad says.

Anu comes back to me and shines his light in my face. I close my eyes. He turns away. I open them.

"We go down," Anu says. He takes his pack off and gets out a coil of rope. He ties the rope round Dad, then me, then himself. He starts walking. We follow.

I hear a noise like something tearing. Anu is falling away from us. Dad's beside me, holding me. He lets go of my arm. I don't know why. He's being pulled away from me, down after Anu. The rope comes tight on my stomach. My feet slide on the snow. I'm in the air. I know I'm going to die. Falling lasts forever. Someone screams, a terrible sound. I land on top of Dad and Anu.

I lie there. Someone's sobbing, big horrible sobs choking out of his lungs. It's Dad. He's afraid.

I have to be a man.

I just have to forget about being sick.

"It's all right, Dad," I say. "It's going to be OK." I don't even know if Anu is alive. I sit up and Dad screams.

Orrie

It's dark. Maybe it's only the snow blotting everything out. I pull my glove down and look at my watch. I can't see too clearly. But I think it's seven.

I have my arms round me. I'm holding myself, holding the heat in. I can't feel my fingers. I've got my hands jammed into my armpits to warm them up. I should undo my coat and put my fingers against my skin.

I hear a cry, in the dark far away. Like an animal howling in pain. Or a demon of the mountain. I cry back.

I hear it again. I'm sure of it. Calling. Stopping. Calling. I hear no words. It's below me, across the rocks. I don't know if it's human. I scream again, a long scream of fear, like a dog.

It shouts back: "Or-rie! Or-rie!"

"Here!" I yell. "Here!" So it'll know where I am. It's not a man. It's too high. It's a woman or a child. Jack. Jack's coming for me.

"Orrie!" he's shouting.

I'm shouting back, "Here, Jack! Here!"

He's coming closer, getting slowly louder. I know I'm

not making him up. Jack's coming. We've always looked after each other.

It isn't Jack. It's a woman. Libby. I hate her for not being Jack. Where's Jack?

She materializes out of the blowing snow, right below me. I stop shouting. She comes on, hunched low over the rock. Her hood and coat and pack are all covered with snow.

She's up to me and I throw myself into her arms. I bury my head in her chest, crying, "Mum, Mum, Mum." My mouth is pressed into her coat and the wind's roaring. I don't think she can hear me. "Mum, Mum, Mum."

She pushes me away, holds me by the shoulders. Libby shoves her face up into mine. Her eyes are angry.

"Orchid," she says. "We have to go down."

"Where's Andy?"

"Down in the tent. All by himself. Because I had to come up and get you."

"You shouldn't have left him. I didn't think you'd leave him."

"But I did," Libby says. "For you. You selfish little bitch." She starts down the rocks. I follow her as fast as I can.

Jack

We're lying on some sort of ledge. Maybe we've fallen off a cliff and stopped on a ledge. If I move, maybe we'll fall the rest of the way.

"Don't move, Dad," I say.

Anu doesn't say anything. I'm sitting on him, too. He's making weird grunts. He's alive.

"Don't move, Anu," I say. But he does. He pulls his body away, pushing himself backwards on his hands. He's crazy. I fall off Dad, between them. Dad roars with pain.

We don't fall. I don't know why we don't fall down the cliff.

I lie there very still. Slowly, I take my light off my forehead and hold it in my hand. Lying still, I let the light play and look around. There's ice on both sides of us. We're in the bottom of a crevasse. The ice floor under us is maybe three feet wide. It's solid. We won't fall any further. I can't tell how deep the crevasse is, or how far we've fallen. The cliffs of ice above us curve into overhangs. In places the curves are the lightest blue. In other places they are clear green, transparent, and hard. There are streaks of light gray frozen water. It's beautiful.

The wind is a distant sound, far above us in another land. We're safe here.

Dad whimpers in pain.

"Stop crying, Dad. Please stop crying."

Anu is still making those grunting noises.

"My leg," Dad says.

I put my light back on my head. I spread my arms and brace myself against both walls. I'm OK. I'm making myself be OK. I have to be. Maybe the altitude sickness is less for even coming down this far. I hope so. These people need me. I look down at Dad. His left leg sticks out below the knee at the wrong angle. A very wrong angle.

I step over him, very carefully, holding myself steady with my arms. I kneel by his feet and touch the bottom part of his left leg. He screams.

"Hold still, Dad," I say. I move my hand up his leg, very gently. He's sobbing, but trying to hold back his tears. My hand finds the break. Dad screams. I think I've touched the broken bone sticking out of his skin. I turn my head away and throw up onto the ice wall. "It's broken," I tell him.

Dad takes a deep breath and says, "I know."

I stand up again and step carefully past Dad to Anu. He's making little grunts now as he breathes.

"Where does it hurt?" I say.

"My chest. I think I have broken ribs."

"Can you stand?" I put out both hands. Anu shakes his head. He kneels and tries to stand on his own. His face is gray with pain. I help him lie down on the ice.

"Sorry," he says.

I stand between the two men, leaning against the ice wall. Dad's crying quietly. I'm OK because I landed on top of them. I broke Dad's leg. Maybe I broke Anu's ribs.

"I'll get us out of here," I say.

"How?" Dad's angry, like I'm stupid. Twenty thousand

feet high, buried in an ice grave, and he's trying to make me feel stupid.

I'll show him.

His pain must be overwhelming everything. I have to forgive him.

I take my headlamp off. Thank God it's still working. I shine it up at the walls of ice. I can see maybe twenty feet up. Then the ice curves in. I can't climb that. But there may be a way.

I untie the rope from around my waist. I back around Dad and pick the narrowest place I can find in the crevasse. I brace my back against one wall. Raise one leg high and jam the crampons into the opposite wall. Raise the second leg and jam it in. Now I'm sitting on air, braced across the crevasse, my back against the other wall.

I use my hands to push my back up six inches. Then I pull one foot out of the ice, raise it six inches, jam it back in. Then the other foot. Then raise my back six inches.

I'm maybe six feet off the ground when my muscles give out. I can't go any further. My legs are shaking with pain. I drop to the floor of ice.

"It's OK, Jack," Dad says.

"It's dark out there," Anu says. "You would never get down alone. Go in the morning."

I won't be able to. I'll be weaker by morning. I may be dead.

Orrie

Libby's ahead of me all the way across the rocks. On the steep bits she goes first, then stands on the bottom, watching me. On the easy bits she charges ahead, then turns round and shouts, "Come on, Orchid!"

We start out across the snow. Her steps are too big. I can't keep up with them. I shout for her to stop. She stops. I catch up with her. "Smaller steps," I say to her back. "I can't do big steps."

Libby's shoulders come up and her head goes down into her neck. She spins around to look at me.

"I'm only a kid," I say.

She lets her shoulders go and breathes a couple of times. "Sure," she says. "You're only a kid. Smaller steps."

It gets steeper. I fall and skid toward Libby. She plunges her ice ax in the snow, holds it with one hand, and grabs me with the other. Libby pulls me to her and we walk together. "Think about Andy," she shouts in my ear. "Think about Andy. He'll die if you don't get down. Think about that. Think about Andy, Orchid. Get down alive. For him. Move. Move."

I hate her, and I move.

Jack

I wake up drowning. I sit up, breathing hard.

"Hi," Anu says.

"How long was I asleep?"

"A little time. We need sleeping bags."

I help Anu sit partway up and get the rucksack off his back. All three sleeping bags are inside it. I zip him into his bag and leave the rucksack as a pillow. He closes his eyes.

I wake Dad up when I try to get his legs into his sleeping bag. He screams, then says, "Sorry." I get into my own sleeping bag next to him.

All night long I keep waking up, drowning. Dad keeps waking up, too. I reach over and put my hand on him while he whimpers. "I'm sorry, Jack," he says. I want to put my arms round him. But I don't dare, in case it hurts his leg.

I don't tell him how sick at heart I am for landing us in all this trouble.

He should have known, though, a voice says in my head.

He did know, really.

Orrie

We make it to the tent. Andy makes us tea. I get out the last chocolate bar and tear at the paper. Andy hands me the tea. Cookie Wolf grabs the chocolate bar. He holds it down between his paws and tears at it. I watch, shaking so hard with the cold that I spill the tea all over myself.

Libby tells me to take all my clothes off, fast, and get in

the sleeping bag. I do. She starts taking hers off, too. I look away. I don't want to see my dad's girlfriend naked. She gets in the sleeping bag and holds me. Libby feels burning hot. I must be so cold against her skin. She says nothing.

It feels good to be held. Andy gives us fried peanut butter sandwiches. We eat them, snuggled together in the bag.

Andy and Cookie Wolf are asleep in the other sleeping bag. I'm terribly sleepy myself, but there's something I have to know. I ask Libby, "What were you and Dad fighting about?"

"Jack. He wanted to take Jack up the mountain. I thought he was wrong."

"You were right."

"Whoop-de-doo," Libby says.

"Why'd he let Jack go up?"

"He felt guilty for leaving all of you. So he couldn't say no." She breathes in once hard, like something's troubling her, too. "Guilt's a useless emotion. It's a bucket of crap. You put your head in that bucket and you come up with a mouthful of it."

"Why didn't he let me go?"

"He's sure of your love. He isn't sure of Jack's."

"Are you going to split up?" I ask.

"Yes."

"Why?"

"I hate weak men."

How can she say that to me? I'm his daughter. It's cruel.

"We're all weak," I say.

Jack

Dad wakes me up again. There's a ghostly gray light in the crevasse now. I get up.

"Anu?" I say.

"Yes." He's lying in his sleeping bag, awake. Alive. Good.

"There's light."

"Yes."

"I'll climb out."

"Walk along the crevasse. See what's at the end," Anu says.

I walk past Dad. The sides narrow in on me. My legs are stiff and still floppy. The end of the crevasse is a jumble of ice blocks and new soft snow. It's steep, but maybe not too steep.

I go back and tell Dad and Anu there's a way out. "I can climb it. I can do it. I'll get help."

"Jack," Dad says.

I kneel by him. I have to listen really hard to hear what he's saying.

"I should never have taken you up here."

"It'll be all right, Dad."

"Don't come back," Dad says.

"I have to, Dad. I'll be the only one who knows where this is."

"You have altitude sickness. You're sick. It will kill you."

His eyes look desperate, gone somewhere to flee the pain. "Save yourself," he says. "Promise me you won't come back."

I kiss his forehead. "I have to come back for Anu."

Dad's face turns red with shame. He forgot Anu.

I get my pack. I need the rope. I untie Dad. His eyes stay closed. I go over to Anu. He's already untying the rope from around his waist.

"Go," Anu says. "Don't come back. You will die."

I pick up my ice ax and leave. Dad is asleep or passed out or something.

It takes a long time, maybe an hour, to climb sixty feet or so. I don't know exactly. I just give my hands and feet orders and sometimes they obey. I rest a lot. Maybe it's two hours.

My head is over the edge of the top. The world is gray, and the wind moans. It's not as bad as last night. But I can't see the rocks. I don't know where we've fallen to. Dad and Anu could never get up here the way I have. I'm not strong enough to pull them up. I have to get help.

I walk along the edge of the crevasse, keeping well back, till I guess I'm just above Dad and Anu. I shout down. Anu shouts back up, "Go."

"Goodbye, Jack." Dad's voice is faint.

"See you later," I shout down.

I dump my rucksack and the rope in the snow so the rescuers can see where the crevasse is.

Orrie

It's wonderful inside my sleeping bag. Libby gets up to go outside and look at the world. She has to dig her way out of the tent with a shovel. She comes back in and says there's two feet of new snow everywhere. The snow's stopped for the moment, she says. But when I look down the valley, everything is white. There's no way any help is going to come up to us for several days. And Libby can't see how we could get down through that snow. But she says it's OK. All we have to do is sit here and wait for Jack and Dad to come down from the summit, fat and happy.

Libby, Andy, and Cookie Wolf are outside making a snowman. I'm warm in my sleeping bag.

Jack

I try to head up toward the rocks. I don't know how far we

fell, but we're way below the path now and I need to get back to it. The climb out of the crevasse did something to me. It feels like some big hand is squeezing my brain. I'm afraid my brains will start dribbling out my nose and ears. All the girls will laugh at me. They'll point at my face and say, "What's that gray goo coming out of Jack's nose?" I put the back of my hand to my nose to try to stop the brains coming out. It won't work. I take my fingers and try to shove the brains back up into my nose. The girls are all giggling and making sick noises. The brains start to come out my ears.

My eyes hurt. I have to close them. I can't walk with my eyes closed. It's the goggles. I put them on. Then I open my eyes. I can see. I still can't find the rocks. It looks pretty steep where I am. I need to head up to the rocks. I should be there by now. Maybe I've gone down too fast, onto the steep part. I'm afraid I'll slip. I won't slip if I head up.

I can't head up. I can lift my feet uphill but I can't lift my body after them. I try to angle up just a bit with each step. I can't even do that. I'm not strong enough.

I want to stop. But if I rest, Dad and Anu will die.

I've missed the rocks. I didn't climb high enough. I must have passed below them. I don't know where I am. I don't recognize any of this. If I turn down too soon, it will be too steep. I'll fall.

I can't go much farther.

I can't go any farther.

I slip and fall into the snow, on my stomach. I'm sliding down feet first. I dig my ice ax into the snow above me. I slide fast, trying to anchor myself. The slide goes on and on. I'm screaming in fear and laughing with joy.

A dog barks.

Orrie

Libby and Andy carry Jack into the tent. I make the tea. Libby takes the cup from me and says if Jack drinks the whole cup all at once he'll vomit. She gives him a spoonful and waits like a mother bird. Then she gives him another spoonful.

Jack looks about a million years old. His face is all sunken and pinched. But he's alive.

Libby tells me and Andy to take Jack's gloves and boots off and warm his hands and feet so he won't get frostbite. I take his boots off. His feet are all white. Maybe he has frostbite already. I undo my coat and raise up all my layers and put his feet on my stomach. The pain of the cold in his feet drives all the air out of me. I let my layers down over his feet and hold them to my bare stomach. I love my brother. I'll probably get frostbite of the stomach and have to have it amputated.

Libby gives him more spoonfuls of tea.

"Where's Dad?" I ask.

"Wait," Libby says.

We wait while Libby gives Jack more slow spoonfuls. Then she gives him a whole cup. When he finishes that, she folds her arms across her chest and says, "OK. Where's your dad?"

A lot of what Jack says doesn't make sense. Everything is all jumbled up, like something is wrong with his brain. Libby asks gentle questions, getting it all straight, making him feel OK.

Dad and Anu are down a crevasse. They're hurt. They need help to get out and back down the mountain. That much I get.

Andy is silent. He holds Jack's hands under his shirt like I've got Jack's feet. I'm pretty sure Andy understands that maybe Dad will die. And that maybe he's already dead.

I take Jack's feet off my stomach and dig in my rucksack for clean wool socks. Cookie Wolf starts licking Jack's bare feet. He can tell they're hurt. I push Cookie Wolf's nose out of the way and put the clean socks on Jack's feet. I put two dirty pairs on top of them and ease Jack into his sleeping bag.

I jam my feet into my boots.

"Where are you going?" Libby asks.

"To rescue Dad. You're coming with me."

"No you're not," Libby says.

"He'll die," I say.

"Jack's sick," Libby says. "We can't leave him. It's starting to snow again. We'll never find them. The snow is too deep to go down the valley. We have to stay here." She grabs my hands. Her blue eyes drill into me. She talks to me like I'm crazy. "If we go up, you and I will just get lost, and Jack and Andy will be on their own. I can't do that."

"My dad will die! You'll let my dad die!" I'm screaming like a little kid. I stand up. My legs are shaking.

"It's that or let his children die," Libby says. "You can't do it. I barely got you down last night."

"You can let Dad die," Jack says. "He said so."

I whirl on Jack. Andy watches us, like an audience. Cookie Wolf has his head in Andy's lap.

"But you can't let Anu die," Jack says.

I whirl back at Libby. I grab her wrists like she grabbed mine. I shake her. "We have to save Anu," I say. I can see her eyes go all confused. "Anu is a good man," I say.

Andy speaks. It's the voice of a child, but he talks like a grownup. "I'll look after Jack. We'll be OK. I can cook. Me and Cookie Wolf will keep him warm. You have to go, Libby."

Libby turns her head slowly to look at Andy, like she's in a dream.

"And you, Orrie, you have to try. Or we're not people," Andy says.

Libby nods. "But I'm not taking Orrie," she says to Andy.

"He's my dad," I say.

Libby doesn't look at me. She's watching Andy, waiting to see what he says next.

Jack speaks. His voice is hoarse and spooky: "One of you can't get them out alone. It'll take two. One at the top with the rope and one below to help them up."

"It will kill your sister," Libby says to Andy.

"That's up to her," Andy says.

"She's only a child," Libby says.

I want to shout: I'm not a child. But this is serious. We're telling each other the truth here. And I am a child.

Libby puts her boots on.

Nobody says anything.

We're going to save Dad. It must mean Libby really loves him.

Jack

They knew there was something wrong with me. But I didn't tell them it was altitude sickness. I don't think Libby and Orrie noticed. They had other things to worry about.

Andy knows. I'm sure he knows.

I told Libby and Orrie about the rucksack marking the spot. And that they have to hurry, or the new snow will cover my tracks.

Andy makes me honey and tuna on crackers with more tea. Then he tells me to go to sleep.

"Dad?" I say.

"I'll wait up for Dad," Andy says.

Orrie

It's snowing again. I can't see much. I knew it was going to be bad. We have to hurry. Libby's leading the way up beside the path Jack made where he slid down. Libby's not that much bigger than me. She doesn't look back once. If I don't keep up, maybe she'll just walk up the mountain and leave me. No. She's not looking back to make me keep up. But she's not going faster than she knows I can manage. She's pulling me up. I love her for that. I don't know what she feels. I watch the middle of her red jacket, right between the bottom of her shoulder blades, and make myself climb. My lungs hurt so much I want to cry.

At the top of Jack's slide his tracks go off to the left. They're already filling with snow. We've got to hurry. Libby waits for me.

"How are you?" she asks.

"Fine. How are you?"

"Fine."

I'm lying. Who knows what she's doing? She ties her rope around me and then around her stomach, leaving six feet between us.

We cut across the hill, following Jack's tracks. We're going sideways across the mountain now, not climbing up. Libby is almost running. Every time she gets even half a step ahead, the rope yanks at my stomach and pulls me forward.

The rope pulls me flat on my face. Libby stops, but she doesn't turn round. I can feel her anger. She stands, her back to me, hands on her hips, drawing in air. I scramble to my feet and shout "Go!" at her back.

I fall again and she waits again, but she never turns round. I get up as fast as I can. I think she's furious at me for being so slow. Furious at herself for taking a child up here. Furious at Dad. Furious at herself for rescuing him.

I understand furious. I can do furious.

I decide to hate Libby. Hate will make me go faster.

I think she's also trying to make me go faster so she can keep everyone alive.

We're a lot alike, Libby and me.

My lungs are screaming. I mean it. The air makes terrible

noises as it goes in and out. I want to stop Libby and say, "I'm only a kid." I don't. At each step, I say in my head, so as not to waste breath, "Dad. Dad. Dad."

We can see Jack's rucksack.

Libby runs, really runs, toward the blue rucksack almost buried in the snow. She stumbles as she runs, clumping into the deep snow. I run after her. She falls, and her rope yanks me over. I yell, "Dad. Dad. Dad."

He shouts back from inside the earth, his voice weak and hollow, "Orrie."

"Dad. Dad."

We're there, by the rucksack. "Anu, are you there?" Libby shouts.

"Yes." His voice is funny but he sounds calm.

"Please, Jesus," I pray. "Please get my dad out."

"Let's work," Libby says. "Take your pack off."

She unties the rope from around me. Then she takes the other end of the rope and ties it round my shoulders and waist. Now we have about three hundred feet of rope between us. I hope it's not three hundred feet down there. If it is, we'll never get them out.

"I'm going to lower you down," Libby says. "I'd go myself but you're smaller than me. I can haul you back up. But first I'm going to lower you twenty feet as a trial. We need to make sure this will work."

I nod.

"Do you understand, Orchid?"

"I do, Elizabeth."

"Libby."

Got her. I smile. "Orrie," I say.

"Stop messing around," Libby says. "We have work to do."

"How do I get them out? They're bigger than me."

"I don't know. Go down and have a look."

Libby has rope over her shoulder and round her back, to brace herself. She feeds the rope out to me as I go down.

The crevasse is narrow. I put my crampons against one wall and my shoulders against the other and walk down. Easy. The rope stops me. "Come back up," Libby shouts.

"It'll be OK," I shout. "It's easy."

"Come back up," she says.

I start walking back up. It's not easy. At this altitude everything's hard. Libby pulls on the rope, yanking me up. It doesn't make much difference. She's not strong enough either. We do it by inches.

When I get to the top, I lie there with my legs across the hole and my back on one side. I haven't got the strength to pull myself up over the edge. Libby is breathing like a freight train.

"It won't work," she says, quietly so they can't hear her below.

"It'll work," I say. It probably won't if Dad's hurt bad, I think.

117

"We'll have to get help," Libby says.

"There isn't any help," I say.

"I love you," she says. Americans say stupid things.

"I love you, too," I say, to make her feel good, and to be kind. I start kicking my way down.

"No," Libby says. She won't let the rope out.

"Dad," I yell down. "I'm coming."

"Orrie." His voice is wobbly.

"How am I going to tell your mother that I let you die?" Libby says.

"Same way you're going to tell Anu's wife you let him die. On the telephone. You'll say you're sorry a lot."

Libby looks bewildered.

"He's my dad," I say.

She starts letting out the rope.

She lets me go because she loves Dad and she doesn't love me.

Jack

I'm drowning.

I wake up. Andy and Cookie Wolf are in the sleeping bag next to me. Andy's been talking to me while I was asleep: "Take the door with the sweet singing. There's a long corridor. Like a big school. It goes on forever. And there's doors all along it. Blue light, red light, orange. Take the door with the clear light. The light that has every other light inside it."

Cookie Wolf has Andy's red wool hat pulled down over his ears. I listen to Andy and look deep into the dog's black eyes. He's listening, too. You think of animals as children. This dog is not a child. He stares back at me, with pity in his eyes.

"Put your ear to the wrong door," Andy says. "You can hear the grownups fighting. Hear the whispers. The hurting. Put your ear to the good door. You hear the mother in love."

"Are you dying?" I ask Andy.

"No," he says, "I'm all right."

"Am I dying?"

"I think so," Andy says. "I've never seen a person die. But you're a lot like Chipper was."

Chipper was Andy's guinea pig who died. There was a long funeral in the garden behind our house.

In my dreams, I hear Andy telling me where to go.

Orrie

I got down here easily enough. Anu and Dad are both alive but weak. Dad has a broken leg. Anu says Jack climbed out at the end of the crevasse. He points to where Jack went. The sweat from the climb is drying, and I'm starting to shiver.

I find Jack's footprints and the narrow cuts of his ax in the snow. It looks steep. I've never climbed anything in my life. But if Jack did it, I can.

I tell Dad and Anu I can get them out. They look at me

like I've given them a puppy for Christmas. I ask Dad, "Can you stand?"

"No."

"Then crawl."

He starts crawling. Each time he pulls his left leg forward he lets out a little scream.

"Goodbye," Anu says.

He thinks I'm leaving him to die. Maybe I was. I didn't even think about it. I love my father too much. "I'll be back," I tell Anu. I don't know if that's true. He doesn't know either. He nods.

Dad crawls to the bottom of the steep climb. He lies flat on the ice, his head pulled back to look up. His face is green in the strange light from the ice. I undo the rope round my waist and tie it under his armpits. I call up to Libby and explain what I want to do.

Dad's a big man. And he eats too much. One leg dangles but the other works OK. He can't do much with his hands. I think they're frostbitten. Jack says that when climbers start to die, the hands go cold first.

I shout up to Libby, "Pull." The rope goes tight above Dad. It hangs in the air, tight and humming. Libby is pulling. Dad doesn't move. He's too heavy.

"I can't," Libby shouts down. "I can't."

"You're going to have to get yourself up, Dad," I say.

He says nothing. His face is still green and lined. His

eyes are full of pain. He reaches his left arm up and drives his ax into the ice. He puts all his weight on the ax, swings his good foot up, and jams his foot into the ice. He hangs there.

"Attaboy, Dad," I say. "Again."

He does it again, and again. The next time he pulls the ax out of the ice, he falls backward. He lands with a crunch and screams.

I have to not care. For him, I have to not care. "Get up, Dad." Hard.

He looks at me like he's never seen me before. I put my hands under his armpits and haul him up to his feet. I yell up to Libby to keep the rope tight at all times.

I'll have to climb alongside Dad, helping him with every step. It's narrow. If I stand on his left, I'll push against his broken leg. If I stand on his left, I'll shove his bad leg into the wall.

I can't afford to care.

I start up on his right, his ice ax in my right hand, my ice ax in my left hand. I kick two footholds with my crampons. I plant my ice ax above me and his ice ax between us, a bit above. I balance on my left foot so he can use the right foothold. "OK, Dad," I say. "Reach up. Grab the ax. Pull yourself up so the good foot is in the foothold."

He does it. His eyes are empty, but he does it.

"Good thinking, Super Dad," I say. "Hang onto that ax."

I take the other ax, mine, and drive it into the snow a foot above the first ax. Then I kick new footholds for Dad and me. I step up. "OK, Dad. Up."

He doesn't speak, saving everything he has for what he needs to do. He makes little sounds, but that's all. Libby pulls the rope taut.

Again. Again. Up and up. While I work on the footholds, Dad leans back, putting his weight on the rope, resting. Libby holds it. She's strong enough for that.

We do maybe fifty holds. It takes more than an hour. My leg muscles are a white sheet of pain. I'm very conscious that I'm not on a rope.

"Up, Dad," I say.

"I can't."

"You can. You have to. I'm not leaving you. If you don't get out of this, I'm dying with you."

"I can't." He cries.

"I don't give a shit," I say. "Do it."

The tears roll down his face. We keep going.

He groans all the time, screams, the breath rattles in his throat. I'm slower. Each pair of footsteps takes a couple of minutes. Or more. Who knows.

"Keep coming," Libby shouts down. I hear her clearly now. No echoes. We must be getting close to the top. The light is different, less shadowy, less eerie.

My right leg cramps. My foot slips out of the hold. I'm falling. I grab Dad's legs. He lets out a terrible cry. I scream with him. His foot comes out of the hold. I think he's lost his grip on the ax. My arms are round his legs. My fingers dig into his knees. Libby has all our weight. Dad howls. Libby screams down at us. I can't hear what she's saying. Dad and I hang there. I want to let go, fall, stop his pain. I hate him for being a coward, for making me save him. I hate myself for being so weak.

I wonder how long Libby can hold us. I think that's what she's shouting about. Only rage will save us now. I crunch Dad's knees hard between my fingers. Too bad if it hurts. I claw my way up his body, tearing at his clothes, kicking my crampons into the wall. Not giving a toss when I bang his broken leg into the wall. He's blubbing, the weakling, the nothing, the father.

I climb past him, pure fury digging my hands into the wall in front of me. I grab the ax, swing it to the next place, and shout at him, "Now. Now. Up. Move. Move. Up. Move. Damn you."

I see Libby's feet and light explodes in my face. "Come on," she shouts. "You've done it."

"Up," I scream at Dad one last time, and we pull him over the edge.

We're safe. Dad is lying down. I sit next to him; both of

us take great whoops of air. Libby puts her arms round my shoulders. "You did it, Orrie," she says. "You did it."

"I'm sorry," Dad says. "Thank you." He holds his arms up, awkwardly, like an injured bear cub wanting to be picked up. His arms paw the air. I throw myself at him, grab him, crying, saying, "Dad, Dad."

He holds me, his arms tight round me, and buries his face in my breast like I'm the parent. He says over and over, "I'm sorry. I'm sorry."

I say, "I love you, Dad. I love you."

We're silent. He's passed out from the pain.

Libby says she's going down to get Anu. I ask her to show me how to belay the rope and make sure I keep it taut.

Libby got Anu up. I held the rope OK. Dad slept. Then we all four lay on the snow and rested.

Dad's awake now. He and Libby aren't talking. But then none of us is talking. We're saving our energy.

"OK," Libby says. "Let's go."

Dad gets up on his hands and knees. His broken bone is in the lower leg. He can just about drag it. Anu stands up carefully, swaying with exhaustion. Libby goes to one side of Anu and I take the other. We hold him up. The three of us start walking together. Dad crawls along behind us.

It's slow. The sky darkens. We didn't love the mountain.

We just wanted to conquer it. The mountain hates us for that. It's punishing us. Big time.

Dad is some ways behind us, screaming nonsense.

"He's not here," Libby shouts back.

"Who?" I ask.

"Jack!" Dad shouts. That's what he was shouting: "Jack!"

"He's down at the tent," Libby calls back at Dad.

"He's dying," Dad says. "Jack's dying." Dad is lying on his stomach in the snow fifteen paces behind us. He reaches out his hands like he's begging. "He's dying of altitude sickness. That's why we sent him down. He'll die if he doesn't get down below Gokyo."

It's true. I saw Jack's face in the tent when we left him. And something on Andy's face. They knew. They sent us back up for Dad, and they both knew.

"Is it true, Anu?" Libby asks.

"Yes," Anu says.

Libby starts crying. Guilt, I think. Dad starts crawling again, to be closer to us. "Go take Jack down," he says. "Anu and I will follow."

"Anu can't walk," I say.

"I will be all right," Anu says. "Go."

"The snow's too deep to get Jack down the valley," Libby says.

"Go!" Dad shouts, lying in the snow. "Save my children. Go."

"OK!" Libby screams back.

"No!" I grab Libby and shake her. "No! No! That's my dad."

Libby lets go of Anu and he sits down in the snow. She turns to me. "These men are dying. Jack is dying, too. We have to save the child. We can't save all of them."

She's talking to me the way nurses talk to mad people. I want to hit her and shriek like a baby. If I do, she won't listen. I force my voice to be flat, normal. "Jack thinks this is all his fault. He came down to get us to save Dad. If we both go down to save Jack, we're leaving Dad and Anu to die."

Libby nods. "It's what we have to do," she says. Anu is right there, lying next to her. He says nothing. He's a good man.

"We can't get Jack down anyway. You said the snow was too deep," I say.

"We have to try," Libby says. "I thought we could wait then."

"If we leave Dad and Anu to die," I say, "Jack will know it's his fault. He'll carry that all his life."

Libby's eyes burn into me.

I say, "If Jack were here, he'd say save Dad."

"Yes," Libby says, "but that doesn't matter."

"Do you love my dad?"

"No. Not right now."

"If you did, would you save him?"

"I don't know," Libby says.

"Save Anu," I say. "None of this is his fault. I'm going down for Jack. You stay and get Dad and Anu down. However long it takes. You're stronger than me. You can do that. I'll take Jack down. You get as far as Base Camp. I'll get a helicopter there."

I stand up.

Libby steps forward and grabs my shoulders. "When you get down to the tent, take Andy with you and Jack," Libby says.

"Why?"

"Just promise me," Libby says.

"All right."

"Say it."

"I promise to take Andy."

"Goodbye," Libby says.

"Goodbye," Anu says.

"Goodbye," I say. "Dad, I'm going to go take Jack down."

He's only ten paces behind me. But I won't walk back to kiss him goodbye. I'm going to need every ounce of strength I have left. "Goodbye," I shout.

"Goodbye," Dad shouts back.

About fifty paces away I turn and look back. Anu is leaning on Libby, standing upright. Dad must be somewhere behind them. I can't see him. The mist is getting thicker. I start walking again.

Why did Libby make me promise to take Andy? He'll only slow us down. It's crazy to take him out into the snow. Libby can look after him once she gets down to Base Camp.

Only she doesn't think she's going to reach Base Camp. I replay in my mind how all three of them said goodbye. Like they meant it.

I scramble across the snow, the fear of hell driving me on.

Jack

Noise. Shouting.

"He can't go," Andy says. "He's dying."

"Too bloody right," Orrie says. "He's got altitude sickness. We have to get him down."

"Who?" I ask.

"You, goofus," Orrie says.

"I want to sleep," I say.

"No way." She hauls me out of my sleeping bag. "Start packing," she says to someone. "My rucksack. One sleeping bag. All the chocolate bars you can find. The water bottles. Nothing else. Get your boots on."

"Where's Dad?" Andy says.

Where's Dad?

"Dad's fine," Orrie says. "Libby and me got him and Anu out of the crevasse. They're following right behind us. But we've got to go. Now."

Dad's all right.

Orrie

I got them packed and out of there. Jack was flopping round the tent. The wind is blowing now, full of snow. You have to bend over into the wind, but you can walk.

I left two sleeping bags for the grownups, in case they make it. I think we're going to have to sleep out in the snow. But we'll all fit in one bag.

I don't know if we'll get through. The snow is awful deep. We have to try. Jack's leaning on me. His arms and legs are jerking all over the place. He's not as big as Anu was, but he's got no control. He's talking garbage about that girl he likes at school, Amanda. I don't really know if he's awake or crazy or something worse. Some of the things he says I don't want to hear.

I don't know where the path is. There isn't any path in the snow anyway. There wasn't any path up here. I can only see thirty feet in front of me. I'm so tired. I have to keep stopping to rest. We're kicking our way through snow that comes up to my thighs. It's so slow. We're shuffling, with Jack's weight on me. That means Jack has to break trail, too. The hardest thing is to get him to lift his feet. But he's trying. He wants to live real bad.

Jack

I can't talk right. I can't walk right. But I can hear what Orrie's saying to me. It's like she's singing a lullaby. The wind is howling around us. "Lift your feet," she says. "I can't do it for you. Lift your feet."

I have my eyes closed. It's more peaceful that way. I shouldn't do that. I have to see where I'm putting my feet.

"Look, Jack. Look," she says. "It's getting steeper."

I trust her. I look.

"Where's Andy?" I say.

"Right behind us."

"Where's Dad?"

"In the tent at Base Camp."

Orrie

It's four o'clock. It will be dark in less than three hours. We can't walk in the dark. We'll fall.

We're too slow. I want to tell Jack to hurry up. If we don't go faster, we'll never get a helicopter to Base Camp. If the grownups get to the tent at Base Camp, Libby will be all right. Dad won't. Anu won't. I think they've lost blood.

They're in shock. They're frostbitten. They were in the crevasse all night. Dad will die first.

Without Jack, I could run. I'd make Andy run with me.

I've lost Andy. "Wait," I tell Jack.

Andy comes out of the whirling snow, stumbling, Cookie Wolf in his arms, like Jesus carrying a lamb.

"Put the dog down," I say.

"Cookie Wolf is sick," Andy says. "Like Jack."

"Don't play," I say.

"You're helping Jack. I'm helping Cookie Wolf."

"Don't play. This is serious. We can't wait for you."

"Jack's slow, too," Andy says.

"Don't play!" I scream.

Andy goes down on his knees and puts Cookie Wolf on the snow. The dog tries to stand up. His head falls over to one side and his legs do splits under him. Cookie Wolf tries to stand again. He's shaking all down the length of his body. He falls again. He lies on the snow, one eye looking up at me.

Andy picks up Cookie Wolf in his arms.

"No," I say.

Andy's blue eyes are very big. He's crying. I go down on one knee in front of him and Cookie Wolf. The dog watches me talk to Andy.

"Jack's dying," I tell Andy. "He's our brother. He is a human being. People matter more than animals. I can't carry Jack and Cookie Wolf. If you carry him, we're too slow. We have to wait for you. We won't get Jack down in time."

I have to make Andy understand. "Dad's hurt up there. Really bad. He's going to lose his leg. Minimum. We have to go down and get a helicopter for him. If we don't, Dad dies. If we get the helicopter too late, Dad dies. We may already be too late."

Andy opens his mouth and sobs. He sits down and puts Cookie Wolf back on the snow. He puts Cookie Wolf's head in his lap and starts to tell the dog about the lights and the doors.

"No. We have to go. Now."

"I got to tell him or he'll be lost in hell," Andy says.

"No!" I scream.

Jack hasn't said anything. Just watched. Now he speaks to Andy: "Cookie Wolf already knows all about the lights and the doors, Andy. He was listening to what you told me in the tent last night. I was looking into his eyes. I saw him listening."

"He knows?" Andy asks Jack.

"He knows. He can find his way."

Andy thinks about that. He bends over and kisses Cookie Wolf. He gently moves the dog's head off his lap onto the snow. The dog lies on his side. In the fading light his white nose and paws seem to melt into the snow. Andy stands up. "OK," he says.

I kneel down and kiss Cookie Wolf goodbye.

Jack slumps down on his hands and knees and kisses Cookie Wolf.

Andy and I help Jack get back on his feet. I don't look back.

It's darker. The gully is beginning to narrow. I don't remember this bit. But all the valleys here get deeper, steeper at the sides, as they go down. So you have to climb up the sides and walk along above the stream, where it's not so steep. But if we climb up onto the sides we won't know where we're going. If we stay down here we'll run into a waterfall sooner or later.

It's dark. We have to stop. I don't know if we've lost enough altitude to save Jack. But if we go any farther in the dark, we'll fall and die. We all get into the sleeping bag.

Jack

I'm a baby. My mother loves me. She holds me in her arms and smiles down at me. The sun shines. Birds sing in her hair.

She drops me in the water. It's bitter cold. I open my mouth. It fills with water. I'm drowning.

Mum pulls me out of the ocean. She holds me in her arms and loves me.

She drops me in the ice again. Andy's singing to me. I'm awake. He's singing "Old MacDonald Had a Farm." He sings "Happy Birthday." I sing along: Happy birthday to me. Andy and me and Orrie sing "Silent Night" together. I hum when I don't know the words. Andy is singing to keep me alive. He sings "Amazing Grace" by himself. His voice soars, and my heart breaks.

Orrie

The moon comes up two hours before dawn and I get them going. Andy wants to pack the sleeping bag in his rucksack. I tell him to leave it. It's soaked through and too heavy. If we have to stay out another night, we won't make it anyway. I tell the boys to eat snow for water. They do it.

The world is gray and cold and full of shadows. Jack's alive but I think he's worse.

It's dawn. We better cut up from the streambed, across the contour of the hill.

Jack

My arm is round Orrie's shoulders. She keeps shouting in my ear: "Go." "I love you." "Damn." All kinds of crazy things. I don't think it matters what she shouts. She's just trying to keep me alive. I don't much care one way or the other. My head keeps flopping over. I'm just slowing the others down. My head hurts too much.

When Mum and Dad yelled at each other I used to go up to my room and lie on my bed in the dark with the door closed. I'd imagine going back downstairs and screaming and both of them being so afraid of me they'd stop.

I guess that's why Dad left. He must have lain on his bed, too. I don't know if I'm going to make it out of here. I'm pretty sure Orrie's lying about that. I know she's lying about Dad. I think he's dead.

Which is my fault.

I have to keep my eyes open and move my feet.

Three

Life and Death

Orrie

The clouds began to lift sometime after noon. We came to the main path. I knew because it looked like an army had passed that way. The snow had been battered down by many feet. They were new footprints. From today.

Andy joined me and we walked on either side of Jack.

I heard the helicopter before I saw it. You can hear the engines miles away in the thin air; the echoes bounce off the mountain walls. It was strange, the first city sound in days. The air seemed to throb.

I ran, leaving Jack behind. Andy ran with me. We came round the corner of a ridge and looked down at a flat space by the glacier. Blue and red and orange stick figures in their down jackets looked up as the helicopter landed. Holding up their arms like it was God.

Andy and I yelled and waved our arms. I took my red jacket off and waved it in the air. No one heard or saw us.

The helicopter landed among the people far below. The blades kept whirring, driving snow into the air. Three little colored stick figures got into the helicopter. Two men helped another one toward the helicopter. They were pushed back, I think. It was hard to see, and the helicopter rose in the air. It banked sideways and disappeared down the valley.

I pushed through the chopped snow of the tracks, leaving Andy and Jack far behind. I had to get to those people before they moved on. Had to make sure they knew we were here, for when the helicopter came back. I was running, choking in air, stopping to shout every ten paces.

They saw me. They waited.

There were twelve men. It took me fifteen or twenty minutes to get to them. They were sitting around in a ring, and one man was lying on the ground. They were all looking at the ground, desperately tired. Some of them, Sherpas you could tell, wore down jackets and boots. Four of them wore thin jackets and canvas boots. They must be Nepalis. One of the Sherpas said, "Hi. I am Sonam."

I was so relieved. It all came spilling out of me, how my father and brother were sick, my father was injured at Base Camp, how the helicopter had to pick up Dad and Anu and Libby. I didn't know if they understood me or not.

"You have insurance?" Sonam said.

Insurance. Who knows? "Yes," I said. "Why?"

"The helicopter only takes people with insurance. They charge two thousand dollars for each person," Sonam said.

"You have insurance?" I said.

"Only members have insurance," Sonam said. I could tell suddenly that he was very angry. I looked around. They were all very angry.

"How do you call the helicopter?" I said.

"On the radio."

"Where's the radio?"

"Members took the radio," Sonam said.

"Where's the nearest radio?" I said.

"Kunde airfield," Sonam said.

Eighteen hours away. If we ran.

"My brother is dying," I said.

"He is not the only one," Sonam said. He pointed at the man lying on the ground. The man was lying on his side, with one sleeping bag under him and another over him. His eyes were open and his breath was irregular. It made a rasping little sound as it came out.

Andy was helping Jack down the path. I went and helped them in.

When we got back to the ring of angry men, no one said anything. Andy went over and sat by the sick Nepali. He took the man's hand and just sat there, not saying any-

141

thing. Somehow he knew not to talk about light and doors.

I wanted to move on. We had to get down the valley. Lose altitude. Save Jack. Find Dad. But we couldn't do it without these men. My body had done all it could. I kept looking at my watch. I tried to do it secretly, sliding my glove back like I wasn't really doing it. I was so ashamed that these men would see me worrying about the time.

The sick man would close his eyes for a while, then his breath would stop and he'd wake up, his eyes big with fear. "OK, OK," Andy would say quietly. The rest of the men sat round in the ring, slumped.

The porter stopped breathing. Andy let go of his hand.

It had taken him an hour and twenty-two minutes to die from when we arrived in the ring. I timed it. God forgive me. I love my father.

Sonam opened the rucksack that lay next to the dead porter. He took out a stuff sack. He pulled a new black down sleeping bag from the stuff sack and held it up, blowing in the wind. "Seven thousand rupees," Sonam shouted. In English.

He pulled out a down jacket, red and black, and swung it over his head, shouting, "Four thousand rupees!"

We all watched, silent. Sonam tore a tent bag out of the rucksack. He took a big curved *kukri* knife from his belt and sliced the bag open. "Thirty thousand rupees," he yelled and threw the aluminum tent poles in every direction.

The other men pulled out their knives and began tearing at the rucksack, stabbing it like it was a man or an animal. Two men sliced the sleeping bag to tatters, and the white down feathers blew away like snowflakes. The men were screaming in rage, no words, I think, and sobbing. And I was sobbing, too, for Dad, for Anu, for the dead man, for myself. Three men were dancing, their knives in the air, laughing with rage.

Eventually it all stopped. We stood and breathed. The men put their rucksacks on. Sonam gave his rucksack to another man and lifted Jack onto his shoulders. The other man was now carrying two loads. A third man took Andy on his shoulders, on top of his rucksack.

"Don't we tell the man about the land of the dead?" Andy asked.

"He's a Hindu," Sonam said. "They do things different."

"Don't we burn him?"

"Hush, Andy," I said.

"We must go," Sonam said, "or more will die."

They were kind to us, those men. I think it was because Andy sat with the dying man. Otherwise they might have left us to die. I would not have blamed them.

The strange thing was that after they destroyed the one rucksack, they made sure they carried all the others. I guess the stuff in them was worth a lot of money.

Partway across the glacier someone lifted me off my feet

and I was carried, too. We left Andy in a lodge in Machermo, the first warm place we came to. I kept telling
Sonam I had to get down to the Kunde airfield. I couldn't
tell if he understood me.

There were new men helping us. We were running down
through the dark, men carrying burning torches held high
in front of us.

We left Jack in Phortse Tenga, the lowest place on the
path. He was fine. Just like that. Smiling, exhausted, but
fine. He was low enough down. He wanted to go on with
us, but the path went up again to Kunde, a thousand feet
up, and I knew he couldn't do it.

We had no money. I'd forgotten about money on the
mountain.

We reached the Kunde airfield, just above Namche, early
the next afternoon. The sun was shining. Yaks were standing in the new snow on the airfield. Sonam took me to the
office and then sat down on the floor and went to sleep. I
told the man in the office about Dad and Anu and Libby.
He said I had to call the British embassy in Kathmandu to
authorize the rescue. He dialed the number for me.

The voice on the telephone was English tea and crum-
pets. His name was George Walters. I told him about Dad
and the helicopter. I felt so good.

"Do you have insurance?" he said.

"Yes."

"I need the name of your provider and your policy number," he said.

I made up a name and a number. "I'll call you back," he said.

I waited by the phone. It was afternoon. The clouds would be moving up the valley. They might already have covered Base Camp. He rang back in twelve and a half minutes.

"They have no record of that policy number," George Walters said. "I checked with London."

"I'm twelve years old," I screamed into the phone. "My father has the insurance papers and he's dying twenty thousand feet up a mountain."

"I don't make the rules," the English voice said.

"Yes, you do," I shouted.

Behind me, a man put his hand on my shoulder. I turned round. He was big, with the round face of a Sherpa, and wore a cap with wings on it.

"I am Captain Namgyal," the man said. "I will fly you up the mountain."

We buckled into the helicopter. Before we took off, he asked me, "Your father will pay for it?"

"My father will pay for it," I said.

He explained that Base Camp was so high up that the helicopter might have trouble taking off with all of us in it. We might have to leave Anu until the second flight.

I didn't say anything.

The flight took ten minutes. Khumbu was laid out beneath us, in all its beauty. I closed my eyes and prayed.

We were up to Gokyo. Pointing because of the roar of the helicopter, I showed Captain Namgyal where to go. The helicopter bucked, rose a hundred feet and dropped as much. It blew from side to side in the strong winds. I thought I was going to be sick, but I didn't care.

Captain Namgyal brought us down a hundred feet from the tent. I saw Libby's head come out of the tent as we landed. At least she was alive. The blades stirred up the new snow so we landed blind. Captain Namgyal would have to hover there. If he fully put down, he might never get back up.

I snapped my seat belt open and leaped out of the helicopter. My feet hit the ground with a jolt. I ran out from under the blowing snow. Libby was hauling a body in a sleeping bag out of the tent. It was Dad. "Hi," he said. He was alive.

I kissed him on the face, said "Love you," and went straight into the tent to see if Anu was alive. He was crawling toward the door. As soon as he got outside I put my shoulder under his and we staggered toward the chopper.

Libby and I picked Dad up first and shoved him through

the helicopter door. Captain Namgyal couldn't leave the controls. The helicopter was jerking up and down. Dad screamed, of course, which was good because it showed he was OK and could still feel things.

Next we hoisted up Anu. He grabbed the floor of the cabin and Libby and I stood under his bottom and pushed. We followed him into the cabin.

The helicopter wouldn't take off. The engine shrieked. The machine bucked up and down. The engine wasn't strong enough for all our weight in such thin air. Captain Namgyal looked at me and pointed at Anu. I threw myself out the helicopter door and onto the ground. I stood up and waved goodbye. Libby jumped out of the helicopter after me. Captain Namgyal took off.

I figured he'd have to come back for me. If it had been Anu, maybe he wouldn't.

The clouds came up the mountain and covered us before the helicopter returned. We could hear Captain Namgyal hovering above the clouds, waiting for a break. Then he went away.

Libby and I went into the tent and took off our boots and got into the sleeping bag to keep warm.

"How did you get Dad and Anu down?" I asked.

"Dragged them."

"Little you?" I said.

"Little me."

Libby held me all night like she was my mother. When I woke up in the middle of the night, I explained about the money.

"Have we got insurance?" I asked.

"Yes," Libby said. "But it doesn't cover winter sports."

"This is a winter sport?"

"Yes." We both laughed.

"How will we pay?"

"I've got the money," Libby said. "I've been saving up to buy an apartment in New York."

"It'll cost eight thousand dollars for the helicopter. More for hospitals," I said.

"I've saved a lot. You wouldn't believe the cost of living in New York." And we both laughed a lot at that, because the cost of living was pretty high in the mountains, too.

"Will Dad pay you back?"

"Half of it. If he can."

"Do you love him?"

"Yes."

"Will he live?"

"I don't know. Probably."

"Are you going to live with him?"

"No," Libby said. "Are you?"

"No. I'm going to live with my mum."

"Come visit me when you're in New York."

I went back to sleep.

We were up before dawn. The sky was clear, and Captain Namgyal was there at first light.

Jack

Andy walked into the lodge where I was staying in Phortse Tenga. He was holding hands with a Sherpa grandmother. "This is Dorje," Andy said. "She knows a lot about yaks."

By the time we caught up with Orrie in Namche, Anu had been flown out to the hospital in Kathmandu. Dad had to have his broken leg cut off below the knee. Frostbite killed his foot. They flew him back to London for the operation. He couldn't get it done in New York because his insurance wouldn't cover it. But the British National Health Service would still do it, Libby said, because Dad had lived so long in England.

Orrie and Andy and I went around and said thank you to a lot of people before we left Namche.

I visited Anu in the hospital in Kathmandu. He was all right. He said they were going to cut off three fingers. Otherwise he was fine.

I was the only person standing by his bed. But the ward

was full of families, talking and joking, eating picnic lunches while the patients groaned. I think they were trying to make the patients feel good. The noise scared me.

Anu said a lot of his relatives had had fingers and toes cut off, and they still worked.

"I'm sorry," I said.

"It's OK."

"It's my fault," I said. "If I hadn't lied about the altitude sickness, this wouldn't have happened."

"I should have stopped you," Anu said.

"It wasn't that simple," I said.

Anu smiled sadly. "It never is."

Dad's hospital in London was all new and shiny and as silent as the grave. He was in a room by himself, and there were all sorts of machines along the wall. He pulled back the covers and showed me where they'd cut his leg off.

"They're going to give me a wooden leg and a parrot for my shoulder, and I'll be right as rain," he said.

He was trying to be brave. I smiled and kept looking at his leg, to show him other people wouldn't have a problem with it either. It was pink and blue and wrinkly, with a big scar where they'd sewn the stump together.

"I never worked with my feet anyway," Dad said.

"I'm sorry," I said. "It was all my fault."

"I should never have taken you up there," he said. "I should never have taken kids up to Base Camp without porters and backup. I wanted to climb a mountain with my children so bad that I forgot about their lives."

"It was my fault," I said.

"You and Orrie saved all our lives," he said.

"It was my fault," I said.

"No. It was mine," he said.

I was standing at the end of the bed, far away from him. We looked at each other. He stared into my eyes. I stared right back. Staring him down. We were locked there.

"I guess we'll just have to forgive each other," Dad said.

I nodded.

"I forgive you," Dad said.

I couldn't speak. I went and lay down next to him on the bed and put my hand on the scar on his leg. He put his arms round me. He was crying. I put my arms round him.

"I forgive you, Dad," I said. Then I was crying too.

Two days later I went back to school for the first time. I got there fifteen minutes early. Amanda was in the playground with some other girls. I went up to her and said, "Hi, Amanda."

"Jack," she said. "Did you climb your mountain?"

"No," I said. "I wasn't strong enough."

Orrie

We got home. I call up Libby a lot now. I try to do it when Mum's not around. I call Libby and then she calls me back so we don't have to pay for it. She's telling me all about men and women and love. I don't think she knows much more than I do, but she likes to talk.

Dad's still in the hospital. He's going back to New York when he gets out. I phone him a lot, too. We don't know what to talk about, so we talk about my homework. As if I cared. But he needs someone to talk to.

Mum's OK. She didn't go crazy or anything while we were away. Her mental health worker comes around every week or so and checks that Mum's eyeballs are still in her head.

Jack and I went up to the Heath together on Sunday and walked by the ponds and looked at the tall trees, all bare in the winter. We nearly froze. It was like Nepal. We didn't speak at all for maybe an hour. Then Jack said, "Friends?"

"Friends," I said.

I'm aware that someday soon I'm going to fall madly in love and it will consume my every waking moment. But I'll always keep a small space free for Jack, my oldest friend.

Mum remembered to give away Muppsells's kittens. But six weeks after we got back, Andy came home with a kitten he'd gotten from a little friend of his down the street. It was black, with a white nose and white front paws. I knew who it was. So did Jack. We went and told Mum that Cookie Wolf had been reborn as this kitten and had come to live with us. Mum said that was a very good idea but we all had to remember to pet Muppsells a lot or she'd get jealous. We said we would.

I made Andy promise never to leave the kitten in the same room with Boa until it was a grown-up cat and could defend itself. Mum said that meant Boa would have to live in my bedroom for a few months. I guess I'll sleep with the covers over my head.

Mum said Cookie Wolf must have been a very good dog to be reborn as a kitten. Domestic cats have the best lives of any living being, she said. They have it both ways. They can go out in the garden and hunt and fight and go for long walks and have adventures. But as soon as they get tired or cold or frightened, they can come into the house and sit in front of the fire on someone's lap and eat canned food. Then, when they get bored, they go straight back outside. And as the cat flap slaps shut behind him, Cookie Wolf will be wild and free again.